TENDER

MARK ILLIS has written three novels and his stories have been published in many magazines and anthologies. He also writes for TV and radio. Born in London, he now lives in West Yorkshire with his wife and two children.

MARK ILLIS
TENDER

To Rachel,
Good Visiting!

Lumb Bank 2011

S
SALT

CAMBRIDGE

PUBLISHED BY SALT PUBLISHING

14a High Street, Fulbourn, Cambridge CB21 5DH United Kingdom

© Mark Illis, 2009

The right of Mark Illis to be identified as the
author of this work has been asserted by him in accordance
with Section 77 of the Copyright, Designs and Patents Act 1988.

First published 2009

Printed in Great Britain by the MPG Books Group, Bodmin and King's Lynn

For Holly and Sam

Typeset in Swift 11 / 14

ISBN 978 1 84471 526 8 hardback

Salt Publishing Ltd gratefully acknowledges
the financial assistance of Arts Council England

1 3 5 7 9 8 6 4 2

CONTENTS

1974: The Last Person to Swim the Channel, Ever   1
1977: Deep Water   14
1984: A Man in Space   26
1989: Being Nice   36
1995: There's a Hole in Everything   50
1999: The Pretty Horse   61
1999: The Realm of the Possible   75
2000: Hiatus   88
2000: Gladness   99
2001: Houdini   110
2001: War and Fish   123
2002: On The Heart, and Other Muscles   132
2004: The Death of a Friend of a Friend   145

Acknowledgements   154

1974: THE LAST PERSON TO SWIM THE CHANNEL, EVER

DAN CAME IN, sat beside the bed like a doctor with a patient, and said, 'I'll be leaving.' The reading lamp was glowing around his stomach, hiding his face in grainy half-darkness. 'I'll be leaving.' Bent towards her, his head at a solicitous angle, his voice apologetic but firm. And that was him gone. Two years in her life, just a cameo role, as it turned out.

Ali heard the door close, lay perfectly still for five seconds, then got out of bed, pulled on jeans and a vest, fetched what she needed from a kitchen drawer, and let herself quietly out of the flat. Down the stairs at a discreet trot and on to the street. A glimpse of his red bomber at the corner. He was turning off Astley Street, towards Grange Road. She followed.

It was quiet, and she had to go cautiously. For a while she walked behind two young men with bulky rucksacks. Their labels boasted they'd been to Hong Kong, Sydney and Amsterdam. She peered round them, just ten steps away from Dan, then was left stalled and exposed as they veered left unexpectedly. Only a doorway saved her when Dan paused and looked back. (Why did he look back? Had he caught a glimpse of her in the wing mirror of a parked car? Or had he sensed her more mysteriously, through some intimate telepathy? Perhaps he'd smelt her; that just out of bed, toasty, seedy smell, mingling now with an edge of something extra. Anticipation.)

A couple arm-in-arm provided her next cover as she stalked him. She watched Dan's back in the frame of their engrossed faces. He was intermittently hidden when they kissed, lips colliding, recklessly moving forward with eyes only for each other.

He was near his flat now, and she abandoned the sickening couple and approached as he fumbled for his key, her stride swift and certain. She let him fit the key into the lock, she let him turn it, then she was behind him, squashed up against him and using her momentum to hustle him inside. She kicked the door shut with her heel, pressed him against the wall. She had perhaps a second of startle-time in which to act. The kitchen knife was out and ready. A long, thin blade, surgical. She stuck it in him without hesitation. There was resistance from his jacket and his shirt, then an easy, lubricated slide. He made a sound like a cough, then sighed, an exhalation without meaning, like air from a puncture. She held him as he sagged in her arms, suddenly mortal, fragile, and heavy. They sank together to their knees, Ali still holding him, and he slumped, leaning on her. They sat together like that while the life drained out of him, and she whispered, 'All right, you're leaving, don't struggle my love, you're leaving now.'

Stop. Stop this and rewind.

She didn't hold Dan sagging, mortal etcetera, she didn't stab him, didn't push him through the doorway. She did follow him through the streets, but briefly, because she was only wearing a T-shirt and a towel she'd grabbed and wrapped around her middle. Barefoot on the cold pavement, shivering, half-naked, feeling almost the second she stepped outside like an idiot. What did she think she was doing? She paused on a corner and watched him cross the road, turn and disappear, oblivious. She stood a few seconds, holding the moment, wanting to prolong it, then she went back to her flat, and back to bed. She lay still, staring at the ceiling, and came up with the sequence with the kitchen knife, worked through it first quickly then slowly, toying with each beat, lovingly crafting the short tale of vengeance and passion.

'Yeah, but I meant it.' She banged the locker door shut. 'I could have killed him. Seriously.'

Steph nodded. 'Good, yeah. Kill him and jump up and down on his grave. But let's swim first.'

'Next time I meet anyone, I don't want to feel anything for him. Seriously. It's my new plan. First sign of passion, run a mile.'

Her toes curled over the end of the board as she leant forward, towards the moment of falling, looking down thirty feet, overcoming her body's fear. She was twenty-five. She could feel her blood moving, as if it was lurching away from the edge. Dan had let a decent time elapse after her birthday, two weeks, then he'd ambushed her. Steph was a small, tilted face in the water. *What am I going to do now?* She was leaning out over the drop. *What am I going to do?* She loved the moment when the fall transformed, as it began, into a flawless dive. Space rushed past her, and she pierced the water's surface with her fingertips and sliced a path for herself deep inside, angling her body so that she rose smoothly and slowly back to the surface, reflecting the arc of her graceful plummet.

She began a steady breaststroke down the pool, Steph trailing behind her. She was no longer any particular age,

3

she was no longer hurt or even female, she was just a swimmer, county standard, maybe better. She turned and switched to crawl, feeling that she could swim for ever, completing the second half of the length underwater where she had the impression that she was cleansing herself of something, where she might have shed a tear or two but it was hard to tell because she was in a world of liquid, and her next length was a flamboyant butterfly, feet joined at the ankles, punishing the water, arms thrusting up from the surface as if in triumph.

She settled into a rhythm, alternating breaststroke and crawl, up and down for half an hour. Ali never thought about much when she swam, but the action of swimming seemed to loosen the jigsaw in her brain, because when she stopped she often found that questions had been clarified and answers arrived at. Steph's ungainly stroke eventually brought her up alongside, and they hung in the deep end, kicking idly at the choppy water.

'I'm giving this up,' she said. 'All this effort for no return. It's not what I want.'

'Liar,' said Steph.

Ali couldn't argue. She only had to catch a whiff of chlorine to imagine herself shaving a fraction from a world record as she stretched to touch the end of the pool, moments ahead of some thwarted Australian. She made little detonations in the water with her heels. 'It's not what I want any more. Everything else suffers for this dream that's never going to happen. Too risky. My new strategy with men, and life in general, is avoid getting hurt.'

She hauled herself abruptly out, climbed on to the low board and threw herself off it, half-slipping, catching her foot on the end, and belly-flopping loudly, slapping the water with her stomach. When she limped back to the changing room and peeled her costume off, she found her skin was raw and red, smarting.

Dan was skinning her. He used a device which, though clearly medical, looked like a sharp, slimmed-down potato peeler. He was careful about it, swabbing each area with alcohol-soaked cotton wool before and after. She lay still, paralysed somehow, while he got on with his work. There was nothing vicious or unkind about it, he was thorough and conscientious, making a shallow cut and teasing the sharp blade into it, then paring long, ragged-edged flaps of skin, one after another.

Ali woke up screaming. Even when she knew she was awake she wept and panted for several minutes, hot and scared.

She turned on a light, lay still, took deep breaths. She'd lost a boyfriend and a lifelong ambition in one day. Was she going to go mad? She felt adrift. She got up, pushed her hair back from her face, and stared at herself in the mirror. Her skin was pale and damp. What path brought her here? She thought how sad she'd have been ten years earlier to see herself now, broken-hearted and sweaty. 'You're a failure,' she told her reflection. Maybe she should swim out to sea, far out, and just sink. Just sink. 'What's happening to you? Are you going mad?'

Her words seemed not to vanish; they hung near her in the silent room.

Three in the morning. Sometimes if she was awake in the small hours she'd read her text books. Sports injuries and their treatments, rehabilitation protocols following various operations, long lists of muscles; all this would soothe her back to sleep. If she ever had children she thought she might call them Trapezius and Gluteus. She'd mentioned this to Dan recently; unwisely, in retrospect.

She picked up the phone, dialled, and her brother answered on the second ring. She could see his arm emerging from under the duvet, the light probably still on, the book he'd dropped when he fell asleep lying beside him on the pillow.

'Is that Ali?' he said.

'How did you know?'

'Lucky guess. What's up, sweet?'

When they were growing up, Frank was hardly ever there. He'd be off on his bike rides, he'd be playing football, or he'd have gone fishing. He couldn't cast properly, sometimes he'd throw the line in underarm, but he loved to sit on his folding seat gazing at the skin of water, watching it dimple and swell. She was drilling up and down the Olympic-sized pool, concentrated effort from her toes to her fingernails, while he was slumped in that seat, head and shoulders drooping, as if gravity was heavier by the river.

'Bad dreams,' she said. 'Dan left me.'

'Good. Never liked him. Want me to come over?'

'You never liked him?'

'Didn't like to say, you being so crazy about him.'

Over the years Frank had metamorphosed somehow, like a slow-ripening fruit, into a good brother. Ali had a theory that it was to do with him being unhappy, and usually single. These two things made space in his life for her. She'd have liked to return the favour, improve his self-esteem, perhaps with a few exercises, the way she could improve the strength of his hamstrings. Ever since he'd disappeared she'd worried about him, felt he was liable to come to harm.

'So, shall I come over? I'll come.'

'No. Don't worry.'

'You come to me, then, tomorrow.'

'I'm working tomorrow. Don't worry, I just wanted to hear your voice.'

They exchanged a few more words, and she put the phone down.

He'd disappeared when he was nine and she was seven. Just abruptly gone missing with no warning, no big row with the parents, nothing. His bed was unslept in, his money box empty and some clothes had gone. After the second night, they began to think he was dead. Posters went up in town, the pond was dragged, and strangely-clad police divers lowered themselves gingerly into the canal. Their mother got an unfocused look in her eyes, and her words came out clipped and harsh, as if it was an effort to let them escape.

Ali shook her head, as if trying to shake the memory loose. At least she was no longer obsessing about Dan. She lay down again, closed her eyes. Slept.

Monday morning, sports injury clinic. Cold muscles used to climbing stairs and getting off sofas had been given sudden, vicious workouts by overweight men who thought they were still schoolboy-fit. Mostly she dispensed advice — sit with the limb up, put ice on it, lift your leg and pull your toes back towards your stomach, warm-up gently next time.

Today, she was less patient than usual. She had a Sunday morning footballer with a thigh strain, lying on his stomach, bending his right leg at the knee. 'My name's Bill,' he said. She resisted the urge to reply *So?* He was her age, Dan's age, the skin of his legs a pasty white beneath copious hair. She yanked his foot down further towards his thigh and he yelped in pain. He turned over and she expected recriminations, but he was laughing. 'Enjoy your work, do you?' She put him on the wobble-board, made him stand on his bad leg, adjusting his balance. 'I get the feeling you're in a bad mood,' he smiled. Then the weighted boot. He patiently lifted and lowered it, testing the strength of the weakened muscle. 'It's horrible isn't it, having to work when you're feeling shitty?'

Men tried to chat her up all the time. They made jokes about bondage, and dominant women. They asked did she get turned on, with all this bare male flesh around? They suggested drinks, dinner, an assignation in the changing room. Before Dan she'd twice gone for a drink, and it hadn't come to anything.

She squeezed Bill's thigh as he lifted the weight, thumbs probing down the length of his hamstring. She'd missed her chance as a swimmer. At her last race, three teenagers had clustered in the changing room, chatting and laughing, and she'd watched their animated faces, the way they leaned in towards each other, and felt her irrelevance. She couldn't match their self-belief. She remembered herself at their age, floating on her back after fifty hard lengths, dreaming of the podium, the interviews, knowing that the next level of accomplishment would always be attainable, with just a little more practise, another surge of effort.

Her words were directed towards his knee. 'No more football for a fortnight. Put frozen peas on it every evening.'

'I don't want to be personal, but are you all right?'

She brought herself back, gave him a lips-only smile. 'Peachy.'

He looked at her for a moment, then they both looked at her hands.

'I'm having a party next Friday. If you felt like it, it would be great to see you there.'

What was his name? Bill. She met his eyes again. Brown, long lashes. He was smiling back at her now, but without much confidence. No smarm at least, no obvious guile. She was going to say 'No', one short syllable to keep this man out of her life. But saying 'Yes' would be braver, would be a sign that she wasn't going to subside into a period of weird dreams, stalking and late night panic attacks. She could take Steph. She could change her mind. She was in charge of her destiny.

'Sure,' she said.

Her hands lay still on his thigh. They both looked at them again, and she saw that he had an erection. *Great*, she thought. *He plays football, his conversation is limp and nervous, and he gets a stiffy when a woman touches him. He's a teenage boy, and I'm going to his party.*

A small package was waiting for her at home. She edged a fingernail under the tightly wrapped sellotape and tugged at it, then got her teeth to it, nibbling at it like corn on the cob. Was it from Dan? What would he be sending her? Maybe a gift. She paused, checked the smudged postcode, considered the size and weight of the parcel. Maybe a red box, containing leaves of tissue paper within which lay . . . surely not a ring? If it was a ring, she'd send it back to him. He'd have to try harder than that, if he expected forgiveness. Arsehole. She went to the fridge, searching for alcohol. Nothing. She only wished she was rich when she opened her fridge. She wanted expensive white wine, good cheese, ham as thin as the notional tissue paper. She had gin in a cupboard, but no tonic, so she splashed some on three ice cubes and returned to the half-opened package.

The torn envelope leaked stuffing on to her lap.

Arsehole was good. Maybe she'd left mourning behind and moved definitively on to anger.

She swigged gin and pulled a cassette out of the envelope. No message, no card, no red box, no tissue paper thin as parma ham, no ring. She put the tape in her machine and turned it on.

'*Dan's a shit and you're worth better.*' Frank's voice. '*Dan's a shit and you're worth better. Dan's a shit and you're worth better.*' It continued in the same way. After a while she fast-forwarded it. '*Dan's a shit and you're worth better.*' It went on for forty-five minutes. She found a patch in the middle where he began to sing it, but mostly it was just intoned, slow and steady like a mantra, over and over.

She'd said she wanted to hear his voice, so he'd sent her his voice. This was like him. He didn't find it odd to sit in front of his tape recorder for three quarters of an hour droning the same seven words, he didn't wonder if perhaps she might find it unhelpful, he just had an impulse and acted on it. She dropped the tape in the bin.

The nine year old Frank finally turned up in Weston-super-Mare. He'd had an impulse to go to the seaside. His pocket money paid for an early morning train, and off he went. He'd only bought a single, and he didn't have the money to get home, so at the end of the day he slept on the beach. He told her if you use sand as a pillow it feels like insects crawling on your cheek. He didn't phone home because he thought his parents would be angry about having to pay his train fare. He told her he was planning to make the money for his return trip; he was going to get a job on the pier, or leading the donkeys. A man on a tractor cleaning the beach found him, and gave him a ride to the police station.

Frank was an arsehole too. How many did she need in her life?

Bill's party turned out to be eight people in a one bedroom flat. Ali had nearly not come. She'd chosen what to wear — short, turquoise shift dress — she'd put a face on and had a gin complete with tonic, and then she'd checked what was on TV, thinking about an evening in. He might be mad or evil, on his own, just waiting for her. He might be really boring. She thought about moving on again. Mourning, followed by anger, followed by . . . what? Followed by diving back into the big world, by taking a few strong, confident strokes in unaccustomed waters. She looked in the mirror to check that she didn't look heartbroken and sweaty. 'Dan's a shit and I'm worth better.' She left quickly, before the dangling words could spook her.

Bill was renting half a house in an unpromising terrace. She could see from his face that he'd thought she wouldn't turn up. He had a brown and orange beanbag and film posters on the wall. *Mean Streets. The Godfather.*

She put her smile on. 'Here I am.'

With her back to the room, she took two quick shots of tequila, just to get rolling. The music was all right, there was plenty to drink, but the people all knew each other, and there weren't enough of them. Perhaps this was the wrong first step, or the wrong direction altogether. What was she doing, giving up her passions? Surely that couldn't be right?

'You drink that stuff like it's medicine.'

She nearly jumped. She turned, and there he was.

'You screw your face up, like this.' He made a face like a walnut.

'This isn't a party,' she said, 'it's a gathering.'

11

'Some people couldn't come.'

She nodded. *Don't nod*, she said to herself. *Speak*. 'What do you do?'

'I'm a writer. I'm working on a calling-card script.'

Ali nodded again, like she knew what he was talking about.

'I need another,' she said.

After that she spent some time talking to Bill's friend the teacher, Bill's friend the student, Bill's friend the unemployed actor. She forgot their names the second she heard them. She told one of them all about Dan, how she'd had this fantasy about stabbing him, not lots of times, just once, because frenzied stabbing would suggest she was out of control and the point of the fantasy was that she was in control. The teacher / student / actor who she was talking to seemed to think that this made sense.

Later. 'The thing is,' she was back with Bill, taking him on as if he'd already disagreed with her, 'you can't know people. You think you can, but you can't. It's like we've been cursed, one of those spiteful Greek God things—you can love each other, you can have sex, you can trust each other and have children together, but you can't ever know each other. Not really, not deeply.'

The music was low, people were sprawled on the floor passing a joint, but Ali and Bill were standing in a corner. She suspected she was haranguing him, but he didn't seem to mind.

'Maybe by the time you're in love and you've had children and all that,' he said, 'maybe you just do know each other by then.'

'I don't know, I doubt it.'

'I don't know either, I've never had children.'

She laughed. 'Stupid. But have you been in love?'

He looked at her, all big-eyed and serious. She thought *Uh oh.*

'I think maybe I'm working on it,' he said.

She began to feel sober. She thought *Here we go. Think of something to say, something polite, ease you both out of this.*

'I'm thinking of swimming the Channel.'

He looked surprised.

'And I'd like to be the last person ever to do it, because it's not enough any more just to swim it, I want it to be impossible for some reason for anyone to do it after me.'

It was a long sentence, a lot of words. She wasn't sure how clear she'd been. His head was looming over her now like the moon. She wondered if she could control her sweat glands.

'I'm adrift,' she said.

His hand touched her cheek. 'Anyway, I think you can know people.' He was almost whispering.

She had to speak quickly if she was going to. She thought, *Maybe it's better when your heart doesn't hiccup and your brain doesn't blank. Maybe it's better.* She didn't speak. His face was aiming at hers. She put her arms round him, and as he lowered his lips on to her lips, she had the slow and not unpleasant sensation of a sea mist creeping over her and around her, enveloping. She couldn't imagine him flaying her. She couldn't imagine wanting to murder him. She tried, but she couldn't.

1977: DEEP WATER

H E E V E N F O U G H T like a dancer. Kicked the fat man in the face, spun, and landed poised and ready to take on the second one. Swayed out of his way when he lunged, grabbed his arm and two-stepped behind him, twisting his wrist so the knife clattered to the ground. Shoved his face into the wall, picked up the knife and suggested we run. That was fine with me.

At that point I'd only been on the island two days, and I'd already put this fortnight at the top of my list of best ever holidays. The ferry had lurched towards the harbour with me and Ali leaning over the rail like we were trying to get our noses over a finishing line. The cool morning sun bouncing off the waves, the little white houses huddling on the hill like sheep. Perfect moment. She had yoghurt, honey and fruit for breakfast. I had a boiled egg with the shiniest yolk I'd ever seen.

'Can we live here?' she said. 'Let's live here and tend goats.'

'I like the way you're thinking.'

We walked up a few winding streets and found a house offering rooms. Fell on to the sheets and dozed for a bit. Made love. Showered, packed a bag with books, towels, sun cream, wandered off and found the beach. Lunch, then more sunbathing, swimming, reading. I watched wind-surfers, their backs arched in grim effort. *No thanks, no grim effort for me, no effort of any kind.* Wandered back to our room, showered and dozed, then back to the harbour for drinks, sunset, dinner. Someone took a picture for us. We held

14

hands and grinned foolishly at the camera. The perfect moment had developed and blossomed, like they almost never do, into a perfect day. It was our first anniversary.

'Congratulations,' she said.

I touched her glass with mine. 'Congratulations your-self.'

'Seriously,' she said. 'This is Paradise. Let's live here. Why not?'

We discussed it as if we meant it, playing with the fantasy, as if we lived lives free of ambition or responsibility, as if every day we spent here would be as good as the one just finishing.

Second day, much the same as the first. In the evening, after eating, Ali headed back to the room, tired, while I decided to explore a little. I don't know how it happened. Two drunk blokes; the fat one called me a wanker. I don't know why—something about me snagged his attention and pissed him off. I didn't say anything, I sneered and kept walking, and that made them angry. It was a dark alley. The whole small town was dark alleys at night. I remember the honey smell of jasmine, the oddness of something so delicate and sweet coexisting with what happened next. The fat one grabbed my shoulder, yanked me round and hit me. I staggered back to see a knife coming out and a third man appearing behind them. I couldn't believe it. I was at the centre of a perfect world, then I was in a nightmare. No pause between the two. But the third man wasn't with them. Kick, spin, sway. Grab, twist, shove. The fight with the syntax of a dance. He acrobatically beat them both up and suggested we run. We ran.

Back on the harbour front, the Mediterranean jostling the quay and whispering, we shook hands.

'Bill,' I said. 'Thank you.'

'My name's Loomis,' he said. American. 'Hope you didn't mind me butting in.'

I laughed, not too hysterically, I hoped. Of course I despise all that — being good at hitting people. Why would anyone learn to fight like that? What would be the point? If you want to stay fit you might as well jog. Of course I envy it too.

'Sure you're all right?' he said.

'Fine.'

We parted. My walk back was fast but stuttery, pausing at corners, hurrying between them, like an amateurish thief.

Morning, and Ali rolled over and smiled sleepily at me. Her hand found my cock and squeezed it.

'I suppose it's another gorgeous day?' she murmured.

'It's starting well.'

I shaved while I told her what had happened. Raking the blade over my stretched skin, thinking about knives. She sat on the chair with the saggy seat, silent until I'd finished.

'Horrible,' she said. She came up behind me and held me in something like a full Nelson, her face on my shoulder, kissing my neck.

'Let's get down to the beach and wash it off.'

I watched faces as we walked along the harbour front. Or, I glanced at faces, wanting to notice but not be noticed. What was I going to do if I saw them? Fat man and knife man. Nothing, probably. But if I saw them in daylight, among ordinary people, ordinary activity going on around us, I hoped they might be diminished.

Sunbathing, swimming, reading. I had a book about screenplay. Three act structure, plot points, conflict, blah,

blah, blah. I said to Ali, 'Aristotle got there first,' but she was asleep. I also said 'You know how long the script for *Walkabout* was? Fourteen pages.' No flicker from her sleeping face. So I just looked at her. Her salt-stiffened hair in Medusa curls and tails, her lips squashed to one side, as if she was deep in thought. The gentle bulge of her closed eyes. The line of whiter skin on her breasts where she'd turned down her bikini. I resisted the urge to put my face into her neck and inhale. I still sometimes got a sense of my good fortune. The collision in midfield mud, the impulsive invitation at the sports injury clinic, her surprising acceptance. She'd told me she wanted to swim the Channel. I liked that, saw myself in a boat alongside, urging her on, handing her a thermos of hot soup.

Her face was suddenly in shadow. I looked up and Loomis was standing in her sun, looking down at her.

He smiled. 'She's with you?'

'My wife, Ali.'

'She's burning.'

Annoyingly, he was right. A scarlet stain on her cheekbones and the tip of her nose. Before I could move he'd shifted our umbrella. He settled in the sand, looked at her again.

'She's lovely.' What was the right response? *Thank you?* He continued before I could speak. 'You recovered?'

'Yeah, yeah, I'm fine.'

I was trying to work out why I wasn't pleased to see him, when Ali raised herself on an elbow and squinted at him. His face lit up with one of those film-star grins Americans have. 'Ali, it's a real pleasure. I'm Loomis.'

A *real* pleasure? Was it a fake one with most people?

She said, 'The guy who saved Bill?'

He shrugged in a winning, self-deprecating, nauseating

way. She eyed him, appraising. Suddenly I knew why I wasn't pleased to see him.

She asked a couple of questions, and he was off on a monologue about busking round European capitals. He'd trained as a dancer, apparently, but his thing wasn't dancing, or music, it was magic. 'Putting razors in my mouth and pulling them out on a string, stuff like that.' Casual, like any real man did stuff like that without a second thought. Ali told him she was a physiotherapist. 'I thought you looked fit,' he said. He was tall, with one of those big, regular American faces, slim and muscley of course, all the way from his calves to his neck. The kind of man you imagine is manufactured by the thousand in some Californian laboratory. Red-haired though, which was pleasing. He'd burn easily.

'Swim?'

He was looking, at last, at both of us. I said no, thinking Ali would too. She'd had a swim just before she fell asleep. 'Sure,' she said, and she was on her feet and they were running away from me, splashing through the shallows and diving into the sea like seals. I watched him struggling to keep up with Ali's strong, effortless crawl. *OK. I could sit here like a lifeguard and watch her every movement, or I could be adult about this.* I flopped back down on my towel.

'Grow up,' I said, to the umbrella. 'You're behaving like a teenager.'

'You talking to *me*?'

I sat up again.

'You *talking* to me?'

It was a short young woman in a small green bikini. Short dark hair cut to the shape of her head. I'd noticed her on each of the previous days. She was going for the big-breasted but boyish look. She was doing an Italian-

American voice, badly.

'No,' I said. 'Myself.'

'Bad sign, hon.'

Hon? I smiled at her.

'I'm seeing two towels,' she said. 'Is that you and a mate, or you and your girlfriend?'

Now I laughed. 'You don't waste time.'

'At home I'm demure and shy, on holiday I'm a disgrace.'

I wasn't sure what to say. I nodded at the book she was carrying. 'What you reading?'

'I'm Bobby,' she said. 'Do you want to be disgraceful with me?'

Loomis and Ali were coming back. She saw me looking, winked and moved on. 'I know you'll think about it.'

Ali watched her go, registered the compact shape, the hint of swagger. 'Who was that?'

I shrugged. 'Robert de Niro.'

Sex that afternoon was weird. I was not thinking about Bobby, and I was wondering if Ali was not thinking about Loomis. In fact if I was thinking about anyone other than Ali, I was thinking about Loomis, which was not at all what I wanted. And did that mean that Ali was thinking about Bobby? What was she thinking? And what if I thought about Ali *and* Bobby, would that be all right?

'Hey.' Ali was looking up at me, puzzled. I'd stopped moving.

I shook myself, refocused. *Forget him, he's nobody, forget him.*

But that evening he was at the harbour, he was doing his act, between the stall selling corn on the cob and the man selling pistachios. Black shorts, black vest, a red sweatband round his head. His hair spiky, like his scalp was on fire. Some spooky music was playing, and he moved to it, one minute shivering like a struck bell, the next shimmying his arms like he was underwater. It wasn't so much that he fought like a dancer, I realised, it was more that he fought like he was performing for an audience.

He swallowed razors, did the rope trick, then picked out Ali from all the tables of watching tourists. He had her chain him up. She held the chains tight while he writhed like a python, almost in her arms, a look of glazed concentration on his face. I'm just sitting there watching this happening. *What's wrong with this picture?* Within sixty seconds he was acknowledging applause, holding Ali's hand, Ali holding the useless chains, grinning. He'd told us he was here for a break, he wasn't going to work. Something had changed his mind.

Inevitably he ate with us, talked about himself some more, told us about little nooks and crannies of the town he'd discovered. A bar where locals drank raki and played backgammon, where to go for the best leather goods, the best olive oil. He talked mostly at Ali. I found myself quiet, watching.

Ali said, 'There's something we need to talk about.'

We were on the bed. I was holding the curtain aside, looking at the swollen, lemon-yellow moon. I wondered if she was going to tell me she was in love with Loomis. Our marriage was a mistake, it had all happened too quickly. She'd tried to warn me, she'd told me you can't know people.

'OK,' I said. 'What do we need to talk about?'

'You know what.' I waited, she sighed. '*Terry the Talking Caterpillar.*'

Mornings I rode my bike around the city, delivering parcels and documents; afternoons I spent writing. Someone had recently passed a noir-ish script I wrote about a murder in Soho to someone else who rang me and called me in for a meeting. She said she liked the script — not really the story, not really the hero, not really the tone, but the peripheral characters, the humour. She said they had a pilot which they'd decided to run with, and they were looking for new writers. Did I want to give it a try? It was a children's show. 'Think *Magic Roundabout* with more narrative drive.' I'd said I'd consider it.

I let the curtain drop. 'The money's tempting, but it's not really why I set out to write. I mean, I don't want to prejudge, but I'm guessing character development for Terry's going to be limited.'

'We all compromise. It's a job, isn't it?'

We'd had this discussion before. 'There's that word again. Compromise.'

'Yes, and that other word. Job. If you're tempted, why not give in?'

Why was she bringing this up? To avoid talking about Loomis? 'What?' I said. 'Don't you like being married to a glorified postman?'

She leant towards me and beckoned me forwards. We kissed. 'I'm not pushing you. I'd hate you to be tied to a job you're unhappy with. Give screenplays another year if you want.'

When someone was being unfaithful, or thinking about it, they were extra nice to their partner. I knew this from countless TV shows.

Grow up, I said again, but silently this time.

I took the after-sun off the bedside table, smeared some under her eyes, and began gently to rub it in. Small circular motions of my fingertips. I said, 'I remember standing outside this shop window, Our Price Records, and a little boy's running along the pavement, his mum trailing behind. She says 'Mind that man!' and I look round, I'm thinking *What man?* Then I realise she means me. I'm eighteen and it's the first time I've heard myself referred to as a man.'

Ali raised one eyebrow. The skin under her other eye trembled. 'Your point?'

'I don't know. One minute you're a kid, the next you're on the way to thirty.'

She shrugged. 'A week after we got married you introduced me to someone: *This is Ali, my wife.* It was the same thing, the same little shock.'

'A good shock or a bad shock?'

'It's another step towards death.' But she wasn't serious, she was laughing at me.

'I love you,' I said.

'Yeah, yeah.' Suddenly she was irritated. 'Where does that get us?' She flopped back on to the mattress as if she was exhausted. She did this, switched moods suddenly. Sometimes it was hard to keep up. 'I thought we were talking about the rest of your life.'

And then in the morning she was gone.

Didn't want to wake you. Gone walking with L.

I dropped the note, pulled on T-shirt and shorts, but stopped myself in the doorway. I'd never find them. I didn't know where Loomis was staying, I hadn't listened to his list of top spots in town, and I felt pretty sure that if he wanted not to be found, he wouldn't be found. Plus, it would be undignified, childish even, to go chasing round the streets searching for my wife.

She'd taken her hat, she'd left me the sun cream. Should have taken it. Ali's the kind of woman who worries about the sun, thinks in the future she'll get skin cancer if she's not careful. Her red cheek bones would be getting redder.

Unless they were indoors. I put that out of my mind, set out for the beach.

The thing is, if there's some attraction there, nothing much has to be said. It's not about words, it's mysterious and tacit, done with looks and smiles. Imagination is involved, seeing yourself with this other person. It's subtle, like magic.

If you're tempted, why not give in?

Bobby was sunbathing near where she'd been the day before. I laid my towel under the umbrella next to hers.

'That really your name? Bobby?'

She turned her head towards me, like there was a lot of effort involved.

'You talking to yourself?'

I ignored this. 'So, did you find anyone to be disgraceful with?'

She sniffed, dismissive. 'Slim pickings. And I'm leaving this evening.' She'd propped herself on an elbow, and was looking me in the eye. 'What are you thinking now?'

I was imagining my lips on her sleek head, the weight of her breast in the palm of my hand. 'Guess.'

'Your girlfriend gone off with the red-head?'

I got up. 'Fancy a swim?'

We walked towards the sea. Blue silk to the horizon. She broke into a jog, then we were racing. She dived, I followed, and we were swimming, splashily and clumsily, out beyond everyone else, out of our depth, out to where the bottom was obscured by dark, swaying weed.

'I get scared out here,' she said, treading water. 'You imagine sharks.'

Being scared and being out of breath, made her younger, less knowing. It occurred to me that she probably hadn't said a sincere word to me since we'd met. Her foot moved

23

up between my legs, rubbed the front of my trunks.

'Getting cold?' she said.

Looks, smiles, imagination—all irrelevant suddenly. It wasn't about those things, it was about a foot rubbing my penis. I'd go back to Bobby's room and we'd make love all day. She'd be eager, loud, reckless. So would I. In the evening she'd get on a plane and fly out of my life. We wouldn't exchange addresses, I'd never even know her real name. I'd find Ali, have dinner, tell a story about getting lost in olive groves, away down that road behind the hotel, twisting towards those blurry blue hills on the other side of the island. Maybe that was the kind of marriage Ali wanted.

I lay on our bed in the cool room, protected by thick walls from the sun's heat. Staring at a crack in the ceiling, listening to insects buzz and chirrup.

Ali pushed the door open, came in and jumped on the bed. 'There you are. You weren't on the beach, I've been looking.'

'You been with Loomis all morning?'

'That prick? I dumped him after a couple of hours, came back, and you'd gone. What, are you jealous?'

'Should I be?'

'He took me to this leather shop, I bought a belt.' She showed it to me, thin and plaited, with a bronze buckle. 'I'll probably never wear it. He had to haggle, very embarrassing. He's one of those men who have to be good at everything, you know? So after that he asked me to come back to his place, and I told him to get lost. That's all, that's it. What have you been doing?'

'Waiting for you. You ready for lunch?'

'Wait, I'll say this. Sorry I got pissed off with you. But what I don't like about you is indecision, always wavering.'

Bobby had said something similar. *Come on, decide. What do you want?*

To Ali, I said, 'I'm definitely ready for lunch. No wavering.'

She shook her head. 'Seriously. You let things happen to you, you let them happen instead of making them happen, you run away from choices. You shouldn't be scared of whatever's coming, you should embrace it.'

Bobby's mouth was salty and her tongue darted between my lips. 'Finally,' she said. But I stepped away, I apologised, told her I knew what I wanted.

Ali was staring at me, waiting for some response.

'I'm going to write the kids' thing.'

'You are?'

'It's money, isn't it, and who knows where it might lead.'

She pulled me off the bed, grinning, all teeth and excitement, like she had a surprise outside the door—a scale model of the Acropolis, done in leather, or the Greek Prime Minister wanting to welcome me to the island.

Grinning like that, she gave my words back to me, like a gift: 'That's right, that's it exactly: who knows where it might lead?'

25

1984: A MAN IN SPACE

I 'M WATCHING THE rugby. Rosa (two) is making a Lego
palace, Sean (five) is banging a jigsaw with a drumstick.
The Five Nations Championship. I'd tried to get Bill interested. 'What a great name,' I'd said. 'Next to the plastic
Superbowl which smacks of kitchen appliances, or the spu-
rious *World Series*—what is that, some kind of soap opera?
—next to them it's almost Biblical. And Five Nations shall
come together . . .'

No luck. Bill's upstairs working, Ali's in the kitchen making soup. So I'm trying some tunnel vision: the kids, as far
as I'm concerned, aren't here. Invisible kids. If Bill was still
here, I'd have told him: *That's what those men have out on the
field, unpadded and bandaged, held in the crowd's open hand, tunnel vision: they have maximum, blinkered commitment. We should
have it too, to the TV screen. Just watch. Watch the wing, watch him,
he's moving when he receives the ball, he's on some unexpected
angle, accelerating, he jinks and swerves and sprints into the open
and suddenly there's nothing between him and the touchline except
shrinking space, and the crowd lets out its breath. Gratification. You
don't want to miss that.*

'Uncle Frank, what are you doing?'

'Mining for gold in Azerbaijan.'

Sean looks at the screen, back at me. 'What?'

'Go and help your mum make soup.'

Earlier, Sean knocked the newspaper out of my hands so
he could tell me a joke. I'd been reading a film review, a
new horror film, and the reviewer hated it so I'm thinking
Yes, OK, this sounds like one to see, and then the paper explodes

26

and Sean appears and tells a Zen joke with no punch-line and starts laughing like a maniac. The really clever bit is, when I didn't seem to appreciate the joke, Sean looked upset. So I felt guilty.

Tunnel vision. But the play is scuffling, kicks back and forth, and now children are on my mind. Children are harmless, they're innocent, and when they're asleep they're quite endearing, but in the end I always wish they'd just mysteriously disappear. How are you supposed to react? There should be a manual available, on how to be an uncle, to explain the trick of it. I know I'm a disappointment. Not so much to Sean and Rosa, but to Ali.

Squeeze the pillow like an accordion, get out of bed and yank the sheet, trying to get rid of the crease that runs up the middle of the mattress. Get my cigarettes, hand one to the woman, take one out for myself, get back into bed and light both. Then realise something awful. I can't remember the woman's name.

'Weekends can be a problem,' I say, as if she'd asked. 'Give me the week. Monday, Tuesday. You look at my week, this week, you're looking at a happy man. Wednesday, Thursday, Friday. This is a clue towards happiness: know what you're good at.'

I tell her I enjoy small, clearly defined activities. 'Like driving,' I say. She's a good listener, whoever she is. 'Films. These are things I'm good at. Watching sport on television. Walking, because a man must have exercise. Observing the life around me. Drinking.' I'm waving my cigarette around like a teacher with a piece of chalk. 'And how have I spent my week? Yes. Driving, film-going, sport-watching, walking, observing, drinking: I've concentrated on the things I'm good at. What I'm getting at, is the joy of doing something well.'

The woman beside me snorts. I look at her suspiciously. She's doing something to her teeth with her tongue. What's that about? I thought she was taking an interest. This isn't the best bit of my week. The best bit of my week was the beginning, in the car, fast, quiet and comfortable, running up the uncrowded motorway on a fine Monday night. The big sky, the lights on the road, the lines racing past. Peace and contentment in my heart. One of those ridiculous moments where things are more intense, where life seems lucid and benevolent and you feel powerful and good. That's what I felt in the car, in the middle of the darkness in the middle of nowhere, after a disappointing weekend at my sister's.

I'm not feeling very lucid or benevolent now, with the anonymous, snorting girl in a hotel room on Saturday morning. But this isn't the worst moment of the week. That came on Wednesday.

'Monday was fine,' I say—again, as if she'd asked me. 'Tuesday and most of Wednesday were fine. There's a tree which is supposed to neutralise toxins in exhaust fumes. I interviewed someone from the Council and a mother of two kids with asthma. I saw the tree. I set up a meeting with the tree man.'

She's almost finished her cigarette.

'What I do is,' I say, (it's as if she's going to sit a test on me, and I'm helping her prepare), 'what I do is, I travel, and I write a short piece on, for instance the opening of the largest shopping centre in Europe, or a man who thinks he's discovered a perfume which turns women on. One editor called me, listen to this: *The Master Of The Wry Smile*. I don't know, I'd rather be the master of the belly laugh, or the thoughtful frown, or maybe several expressions, but I suppose it's something.' I decide to risk a question. 'It's something, isn't it?'

She just yawns. She has large eyes in a thin face. Nice cheekbones. Hardly any lips. If she smiled, she might look attractive. When she frowns, she just looks thin.

I try another question. 'Shall I order breakfast?'

She shrugs, so I do.

'Wednesday evening,' I say, when I've put the phone down. 'Everything's going fine and I need a break. So I'm in the queue, the cinema queue, in the big, bright foyer, smelling popcorn and sweets, when I notice this crowd of girls. Nothing seedy about it, just observation. How they behave and what they're doing. I do this, this mental sizing up. Over the years I've spent hours on it, and I've come to a conclusion: we're all more or less the same.'

She looks at me. For a moment I think she's going to say something. Her lips part, a nostril flares slightly. But she doesn't. Speech is apparently too much effort, and she looks away again. So I continue. Why not? She hasn't told me to stop.

'Most of us have families, most of us have kids, and if we don't we have feelings towards each other, relationships, we all feel rage in traffic jams, and feel helpless with technology, and feel inadequate with the general business of coping with life. Am I right? And I could go on. I made a list once, and I only stopped because it got tedious.'

I say the word *tedious*, and she suddenly gets out of bed. I watch her, naked, head for the bathroom.

'Strip us naked,' I say, but softly, so she won't hear over the bathroom's fan, 'and we all have the same physical sense of being in the world, of carrying the weight of our bodies, their droops and sags and swellings, of feeling hot and cold and hungry and tired. And as our bodies become less reliable, we all become increasingly aware of death. How can we not share at the very least a sense of the precariousness of being alive?'

That's as close as I come to a philosophy. But then I see the crowd of girls in the cinema. All in their girl-costumes: short skirts and strappy tops and long heels, stiff hair, arms tightly folded because their thin clothes leave them cold, chattering in conversations that aren't important but are sometimes hilarious. Just some girls, like a glamorous freemasonry, flaunting their codes and signals, but looking at them I'm finding it hard to convince myself that they and I have much in common. Their bright colours, their physical slightness, their mutual understandings. Perhaps I was just feeling susceptible, but on that Wednesday evening, at that particular moment, I found all my thoughts on the subject being turned around.

She comes out of the bathroom. Still naked, no towel round her. What I'd like is for her to get in bed and get on top of me and shut me up with a deep, firm, sympathetic kiss. Her clothes are piled on a chair.

'The implications are far-reaching,' I say, as if she's not naked, 'and I've not worked them out yet, but they relate to how we as individuals stand in the world, where we are, and how much alone we are in the world. Stay for breakfast.'

She's pulling on her T-shirt and her knickers.

'Please?'

She stares at me, takes another cigarette from my packet, moves her clothes on to the bottom of the bed, and sits down on the chair. I smile at her. She rolls her eyes.

The moment in the cinema foyer wasn't the worst

moment, but after it the film was a relief. Ali can't work out why I like horror films. It's not difficult. I like blood and flesh splattered all over the screen. I like gleaming metallic figures, monsters with claws and teeth, darkness and fog and charming, smiling madmen. I like lives turned upside down, and the business of living reduced to just staying alive. I like to see layers of civilised behaviour stripped away to reveal, we're back on this point again, to reveal the basic human instincts that we all share.

'Eating is one of the loneliest things I do,' I say. Maybe I'll win her over with my honesty. 'But on this evening, when I walk in to the place, the first thing I see is one of the girls from the queue. Only now she's alone she's a young woman, not a girl, still probably ten years younger than me, but she looks older than she did, and she doesn't look quite so foreign, quite so different, so after a bit of arguing with myself, I approach her, where she's sitting alone with a drink. We had a conversation.'

I say I saw her at the cinema, and I ask if she enjoyed the film. She says she did. It's not scintillating stuff, but it felt fine to make a human connection in the drifting middle of the week. The film gave us something in common, so that meant there was a sameness between us. (One of the things about sport, I've tried to explain to Ali and Bill, is that you're part of a group of people and you have this thing in common, this passion about what's happening on the patch of grass down there, and you care about it together. You all gasp or yell or sing or rise to your feet together. The crowd swallows you and digests you.)

'We had the film in common, and the conversation picked up a little, but what we said isn't the point. We got on, that's the point. We chatted, we were likely to exchange phone numbers, which means we enjoyed each other's company, and we might call each other, meet again, for more talking, perhaps for a meal, another film, then sex, then God knows what, marriage maybe, all springing from this chance conversation about a mediocre horror film. But what we said isn't the point, the point is that after twenty minutes, came the moment. I go to the bar to get more drinks — it's crowded by now and almost as soon as I stand up I can't see her — I went to go to the bar, but I find myself instead going in a different direction, I find myself instead walking out of the place.'

She's staring at me again, feet up on the corner of the bed, looking puzzled.

'You're wondering where you fit into this, aren't you?' She raises her eyebrows.

'Well, to be honest, when you meet in a club and you're both off your faces, it's a completely different sort of transaction, isn't it?'

I hold my breath, expecting her at this point to leave. She laughs. And she does look more attractive. She should try it more often.

'Children get relationships,' I say, encouraged. 'They know when there's no connection between them and you. There's a ruthlessness about them. After a while they don't try to involve you any more, you become irrelevant.'

The woman seems to be fascinated by the end of her cigarette.

'I'm saying when I left the table I felt unconnected to this young woman. Even though I was the one leaving, I felt rejected.'

I've asked myself why I walked away. I've also asked myself why, given my thoughts about children, I'm going to Ali's for the weekend again. Presumably because the young woman was the wrong person and there are times when you need the right people around you, even if you don't seem to be quite relevant to them, because you find that you're suffering from something which steals upon you like the symptoms of a disease: a sense of the distance between your skin and everything else in the world.

That's what I missed, back in my room that Wednesday night. Feeling her body along the length of mine, the smell of her flesh, her hair. Not sex, proximity.

'It's quite rare, but sometimes you can pinpoint the exact moment when something went wrong, and as a result everything that followed was not what it should have been. Simple: I left the bar, and then my evening fell apart.'

She glances at her clothes. That laugh of hers seems a long way away now. I swivel out of bed.

'I'm going to have a wee.'

I stand in the bright, white tiled space, watching the thick, dark yellow stream. I'm thirsty. I look in the mirror, to see what the nameless woman has been seeing. Curly hair grown too long. I look like Harpo Marx. Squashed, bloodshot eyes, floury skin. But I don't think of the nameless woman presented with this sight, I think of Ali, of the inevitable questions I'll face this weekend.

Yes, (I'll tell her) *I do sometimes meet women.*

The problem, (I'll tell her) *is identifying the right one. The right relationship.*

No, (I'll tell her) *my demands are not unreasonable.*

(My demands: she should find it possible to tolerate the things about me that need tolerating; she should occasionally say something without looking at me, then turn to me and smile; she should suggest feasible answers to several questions that puzzle me; she should like Ali and her family, but not too much; she should not want children.)

Obviously, I won't tell Ali that when I look at Sean and

Rosa I wish they'd disappear. I won't tell her what I suspect to be the case. That there are areas in which I cannot function. It's not sex, I can accomplish that all right. It's the difficulty of knowing someone, of being with them, of becoming related to them. There are things I do well, and things I don't do at all.

When I come out of the bathroom, Anita's gone, of course. *Anita.* Perhaps if I'd used her name she would have spoken to me. There's a knock at the door and I go to it quickly, with a towel round my middle. Is she back? No. A smiling man has two breakfasts on a tray. I thank him, and when he's gone I drink a glass of orange juice quickly, then pour a cup of coffee.

I never got to finish the story. The rest of that sleepless Wednesday night I spent adjusting pillows and sheets but not getting comfortable, arguing with Ali in her absence, and then looking back, over years, over a lifetime, miles away from sleep now, to find the crucial moment where things slipped out of the groove and everything started to get a bit foggy, a bit difficult, a bit less than natural. Of course, I didn't find that moment, you can't possibly find it, but you feel it, you feel the knowledge that you've made a mistake that you're still paying for, and will always inevitably be paying for. It may be something very small, the difference between doing something and not doing it, between taking a step and not taking it.

Watch the wing.

He's in space, he can see his path ahead of him, around the people in his way, it's going to be perfect, and the ball like a divine gift is coming towards him, it's in the strange, milky glare of spotlights, over the shining grass the ball flies to him and he reaches out for it, properly grateful, and then something happens, something does not connect, his hands flap over it, seem almost to beat it away, and he drops it. *That* is the moment when it's too late. All that remains is the endless process of regret. The movement of the game continues, and he moves with it, but part of him is still standing there, where the ball was dropped, replaying the damaged moment, the small death, the moment that denied him the perfect path ahead, so that it will never be taken, or will perhaps be taken by some other person, but not by him, not by him.

1989: BEING NICE

Janice has weird teeth. She's got a brace, but they're still weird. The two top-front ones stick out in different directions. Even if she closes her mouth you can tell her teeth are funny, because it looks like she's sticking her lips out. Everyone calls her Rabbit. She used to argue about it and get angry or cry, but she's just given up now. Someone says 'Rabbit,' and she just turns round and says 'Yes?' No one says it much anyway, because no one likes her much.

I got to the meeting late. Everyone was standing in the hall in a big group, shuffling and whispering. Boulton was on the stage and Janice was standing a bit separate from the group, watching him.

'Hey, Sean!' Nathan waved and beckoned me over. I don't know why I did what I did next. I walked right past Nathan and went up to Janice. I said 'Hello, Rabbit.'

Except maybe I do know why I did it. All anyone's been going on about for weeks and weeks is my sister. She did an IQ test where you're supposed to score about a hundred, and she scored about two hundred and fifty or something. So suddenly they know why she's not doing well at school — it's not because she's stupid, it's because she's bored. So it's all: *Let's bump Rosa up a year*, or *Let's find special teachers*, or *Let's all move so we can be near some special school for misfits*. And I'm like, *Hello? I am still here*. And when nobody listened and nobody listened and nobody listened to anything I said, I pushed Rosa over. I didn't push her down the stairs. I did

36

TENDER

not push her down the stairs. But I did push her over near
the stairs, and she did fall down some of them. Not even all
of them, just some of them.

And that's why when Nathan said 'Hey, Sean!' I went to
talk to Janice. Because my mum's so angry with me and
thinks I'm horrible. Which I can tell from the way she looks
at me at the moment: puzzled and cross and with her lips
almost disappeared. *This proves I'm not horrible,* I thought as I
went over, and I said 'Hello, Rabbit.' She looked at me, suspicious. Then Boulton stopped walking up and down the
stage, said 'Be quiet, peasants,' and started telling us about
the play he'd written that we were all going to be in.

'It's a musical,' he said. He wasn't shouting but his voice
was filling the hall. That's a trick some teachers have.
'Think *Top Hat*,' he said, stretching his hands out and kicking the floor with his toes. 'Think *The Wizard of Oz*, with just
a smatter of *Saturday Night Fever*.' Now he had one hand in
the air, and he was clicking his fingers. 'The thing about
musicals is heightened reality, which means they're like
your grubby little lives only sprinkled with stardust. No one
breaks into song in real life, no one hears an orchestra
swelling up as they stroll down the High Street. But musicals give you an escape, they're like a doorway, through
song, into a a life lived according to different rules.' He
looked around at us, looking up at him. 'OK?'

There was a silence that meant no one knew what he
was talking about. He didn't seem to mind. He put his
hands in his pockets, a bit swaggery. His stomach stuck out
and his blue shirt looked tight.

'Now,' he said, 'who can sing?'

There was a different kind of silence, one you could
almost feel. It settled around the hall, like something
scratchy and uncomfortable. No one put their hand up.

37

Boulton nodded, like he'd expected this. 'We'll see,' he said. 'We'll see.'

What happened next was terrible. We all had to line up and one by one sing 'Frère Jacques'.

'I hate this,' Janice whispered.

'Me too.'

'I can't sing.'

'Me neither.'

'Why did you say hello to me?'

I shrugged. 'Shall I call you, Janice?' I said.

She stared at me. She had a small face and wavy, light brown hair the colour of butterscotch. Nathan was singing *Dormez vous, dormez vous* in a voice like the squeaky hamster we used to have in Year Two. Janice shrugged back at me. Then she nodded.

We got our parts. I was the burglar, she was aunt Betty. I was going to rob her, but she woke up and kept me talking until Syd and Carly came and rescued her. They did this by singing a song together while throwing a lassoo over me made from the belt off a dressing gown. Boulton called this heightened reality, I call it stupid. The bad part was letting Syd and Carly beat me up, the good part was that me and Janice didn't have to sing anything. We must both have sounded even worse than Nathan when we did 'Frère Jacques'. No doorway into a life with different rules for us.

Mum was waiting outside as usual.

'I'm going to be the burglar, and Janice is aunt Betty, this is Janice, can she come home for tea?'

'Why's Rabbit here?' Rosa ran up to join us.

'Rabbit?' said Mum.

Rosa was looking at her teeth. 'Everyone calls her Rabbit.'

'Her name's Janice,' I said.

Janice just looked at us, one by one as we spoke, her mouth closed and her lips sticking out even more than usual.

'Hello, Janice,' said Mum. 'Would you like to come back for tea?'

Rosa showed off. We were eating in front of the television. She said she wanted something else on, she said I was eating too loudly, she told Janice how clever she was, how hardly anyone in the whole country got her score on the IQ test.

'You're not clever,' I said. 'You think you're clever?'

She smiled, like she'd just been waiting for this, turned to Janice and delivered the trump card she'd been saving. 'He pushed me down the stairs.'

Janice stared at her. She'd hardly spoken since she arrived. 'Don't blame him,' she said.

I laughed, then swallowed my toast the wrong way and had a coughing fit. Janice started laughing too, not at what she'd said but at the reaction she'd got from me. Her laugh was a big, pleased, hicuppy sound that I'd never heard from her before. After that we ignored Rosa completely and talked about our big scene. Rosa kept trying to interrupt, she asked about the play, about our parts, but we just pretended she wasn't there until finally she went up to her room in a strop.

Mum and me drove Janice home, and when she'd gone Mum asked me about her. 'I haven't heard you mention her before.'

'No one likes her,' I said. 'But she's in the play with me, so I just said hello.'

She was smiling at me. She hadn't smiled at me for days. 'That was nice of you,' she said.

Yes, it was, it was nice of me. I'd impressed her. I'd

impress Dad too if he was ever around. I smiled back at Mum with my modest, nice, bright-but-not-brilliant, eldest child smile. As soon as we got back home we heard Rosa's door slam, like she'd been waiting for us to walk in before she did it. I went off to do some homework. Today had been a good day.

Janice sat up in the bed while I stood beside her, wondering what to do with my arms. If they were behind my back it felt too formal, if they hung at my sides they felt heavy and strange. I folded them. Boulton was waving his around, pointing from me to Janice and back to me, then making a sort of flowing movement with his hand in front of his mouth.

Pointing at Janice: 'You talk to him, you say' (his voice went high-pitched and weak): '*Why are you doing this? You don't have to be a burglar.*' Pointing at me: 'And you say to her' (deep and gruff) '*What do you know about my life?*' His hand opening out in front of his mouth. '*Maybe burgling's all I'm good at, maybe it's my metier.*'

'My what?'

'My metier. What are you doing with your arms? Unfold them. It means it's what you're best at. Cross out *metier* and just say *maybe it's what I'm best at.* And then there's this long speech, where you tell her how you became a burglar, and she starts to trust you, and then you kiss her.' He went quiet suddenly, looking at the script. I was not looking at Janice and she was not looking at me. She was blushing though, I could see from the corner of my eye. I picked up my script off the bed and looked at that instead.

'I'm having second thoughts,' Boulton said. 'Maybe we don't need you telling her how you became a burglar.'

'It's my big speech.'

Janice objected too. 'I like what she says here, *You're melting my heart*. That's sweet.'

'It's all fine writing, but the essence of drama is economy. I think you can just say that line, about it being what you're best at, and then you can kiss her. Or maybe touch her cheek, sort of brush it with your fingers in a wistful way, then you're just about to kiss her, and that's when Syd and Carly, you come in.'

'He doesn't kiss me?'

'This is better. We cut the dead wood, and we have him almost kissing her, and then you're interrupted.'

'Narrow escape,' Syd whispered to me, as he came on stage.

'I know,' I whispered back, and immediately felt guilty. That wasn't nice.

Janice's mother had ordinary teeth. She was wearing a red and white checked shirt and she'd made some biscuits. She also had a really nice smile and looked like she'd never in her life thought anyone was horrible. She said Janice had told her all about me, and she was looking forward to seeing us on stage together, and it was a shame our lines had been cut. I nodded and smiled at her so she'd smile at me again, wondering if Janice was adopted. Maybe Janice's dad had weird teeth and nobody liked him.

We went upstairs. Sometimes, when I go into my bedroom, I can smell yesterday's gym kit, or dirty socks. Janice's room smelt like a new box of tissues. She sat on the bed. 'Right,' she said.

We started rehearsing the original version of our scene. I told her how I'd become a burglar (basically it was all down to my terrible upbringing), she told me I was melting her heart. I sat on the bed and leant towards her, then straightened quickly.

'Then I'll kiss you,' I said.

'Then you'll kiss me,' she agreed.

We sat there for a minute. She had a couple of jigsaws in her room, a lot of soft toys, and some board games I didn't like the look of. I couldn't leave yet, her mum would wonder why I was going, so instead I told Janice about Rosa. How I didn't actually push her down the stairs; how she was getting all the attention; how anyway she only fell down a few stairs, not all of them. Janice was good at listening. She looked at me and nodded and made sympathetic noises. So I kept going. I told her how sometimes Rosa and me would sit at the top of the stairs and listen to my parents arguing; how Mum giving up her job had got Dad worried; and how once one of them had thrown something, a plate we thought, but we weren't sure who'd thrown it and who it had been thrown at, because in the morning it was all swept up and not talked about. She didn't actually say I was melting her heart, but her eyes were big in her small face and they were fixed on me the whole time.

Downstairs again, I went into the kitchen for a drink and Janice's mum put her hand on my shoulder.

'Janice isn't very happy at school.'

I wasn't sure what to say to this, so I looked at the taps over the sink.

'She's not very popular is she?'

Direct question—I had to do something. I shrugged, my shoulder lifting into the palm of her hand. One of the taps was dripping.

'I don't want to embarrass you, Sean, but I'm glad she's got to know you.'

So it was official: I was a nice person. My mother and Janice's mother both thought so, and mothers are experts on these things.

Loneliness sounds like the wheel turning in a hamster's cage.
Loneliness looks like a playground with no one in it.
Loneliness feels like an old book.
Loneliness tastes like cabbage.
Loneliness smells like cabbage.
Loneliness says: Where have you all gone?
It was Thursday. Usually I'd have started thinking about the weekend by now, but mostly I was thinking about the play, and Janice. Where was being nice getting me? It was just making life complicated. Boulton sat behind his desk, reading something. Biros tapped and slid on exercise books, someone coughed, and beside me Nathan sighed.
'What have you got?' he said, looking over my shoulder.
'Loneliness.'
'I've got Rage. This is stupid.'
'I know.'
'What's the point of this?'
All the teachers had their things. Mr Turner had a glass eye, Mrs Jenkins was small and Welsh and called you dunderhead, Miss Horne had big breasts and Mr Boulton called everyone 'peasant'. When Nathan said *What's the point of this?* Boulton looked up from his book, took off his gold-rimmed glasses, and stared straight at me.
'Did you speak, peasant?'
'No,' I said. Nathan had his hand over his mouth. He was trying not to laugh.
'Stand up.'
Mostly, life moves along without me noticing. Things

just happen, or I just do things without thinking because I want to do them (go for a bike ride), or because I have to do them (the washing-up). Mostly, I don't actually have to choose anything. Life moves along and I move along with it. Lately though, life seemed to be all choices. I'd chosen whether to push Rosa, I'd chosen to speak to Janice and rehearse with her, now I had to choose whether to rat on Nathan.

I stood up. 'I was just wondering,' I said, 'why we were doing this.'

He stood up too. Hands in pockets again, stomach sticking out.

I got away with a short lecture, a lot of sarcasm, ('Perhaps you'd like to teach the class? Perhaps you're not interested in words and language?'), an apology, and having to get up in front of everyone and read out my piece. ('Why cabbage?' Boulton said. I shrugged. 'I don't like cabbage.' He sighed.)

'Nice one,' said Nathan, at break. 'Want to come back to mine after school?'

'I can't.'

'Why not?'

'We've got the play next Wednesday, I have to learn my lines.'

'You've got hardly any lines. Come back to mine.'

I shook my head. I was going to Janice's house again, to eat her mum's biscuits and work on my big speech with her.

It was like Nathan read my mind. 'You going to be with Rabbit?'

'What?'

'Rosa said you've been going round to her place. You love her, don't you?'

'Shut up.'

'Sean loves Rabbit,' he sing-songed. 'You going to have some baby rabbits with her?'

I wanted to hit him. I also wanted to hit Rosa. My right hand was in a fist. Instead I said, 'Rabbit's ugly.'

He said 'Duh.' Then he said 'So are you coming round mine, or what?'

'Yeah,' I said. 'Why not?'

Janice sat at my table at lunchtime. Nathan was sitting about three people away from me. She gave me a big smile, as if she wanted to show me her teeth. I nodded at her, and started to eat my lunch as fast as I could. 'Can't come tonight,' I said, my voice muffled by a mouthful of mashed potato. Her teeth disappeared. I was surprised how quickly that suspicious look came back into her eyes. She'd been used to being suspicious for years, she hadn't been used to being friendly for very long. I glanced around. Everyone else seemed to be talking about football or TV or the Maths test we had coming up.

'Friday?' I said.

Her smile reappeared. 'Yes, Friday.'

I bolted the rest of my food and moved away. I'd managed to deal with Nathan and I'd just about managed to be nice to Janice, now I wanted to find Rosa. I wasn't planning to be nice to her.

'You don't fool me.' Her face was screwed up, as if she was the one who had a right to be angry. 'You don't really like Janice, you're just trying to please Mum.' I'd confronted her in the playground, but she'd started on me before I could open my mouth. 'Tell me you like Janice. Go on, tell me you like her.'

I stared at her. She looked ferrety with her face screwed up like that. I'd have told her so, I'd have called her all sorts of names, I might have explained to her about being nice, and I'd certainly have found an answer to her question and left her speechless and embarrassed, but the bell went at that moment so I just walked away from her, not too quick, I just walked away.

Went to Nathan's Thursday evening. Went to Janice's Friday. Played video games with Nathan, ate home-made biscuits and explained how I'd become a burglar with Janice. She told me I was melting her heart. I did something I hadn't expected. Janice was sitting up on her bed. 'You're melting my heart,' she said. We both hesitated. She started to say *This is where you'd kiss me*, but she'd only got as far as 'This' when I kissed her. I bent, my lips touched her cheek, I straightened again. She stared at me. 'Then Syd and Carly will come in,' I said. She agreed: 'Then Syd and Carly will come in.' I looked at my watch, told her it was time I went, and then went. Her mum was downstairs, wearing a red top with a zip at the neck. She said goodbye without looking at my lips.

The weekend happened. Bike ride, supermarket, TV, homework, private rehearsal. I gave my big speech to my reflection. Sunday morning, I walked into the bathroom and found Dad shaving, so he showed me how to do it. Mum came in and found me with cream all over my face and we all laughed. The nice family. Rosa and I didn't speak to each other, but somehow without speaking she kept saying the same thing every time she looked at me. *Tell me you like her.* Monday went by. Janice sat next to me at lunch again. Nathan said 'How's your girlfriend?' Tuesday went by. We had a dress rehearsal and Janice and I stuck to Mr Boulton's shorter version. Even doing the short version, just saying *Maybe burglary's all I'm good at*, and touching Janice's cheek, people laughed at me when I went back-stage after my scene.

Wednesday came. First night. My parents and Janice's parents were there. About a hundred other parents were there. Most of the teachers were there. Mr Boulton wore a shiny green suit. Most of my friends were there, either on stage or in the audience. It all began with a song about being hopeful and persevering. (*If what you feel in your heart is fear, Then persevere, persevere!*) This involved the whole cast, me and Janice included, although we'd been told to only mouth the words. We stood at the back, opening and shutting our mouths. I wondered what she was thinking. I wondered what I was going to do. I squinted into the lights, trying to make out faces. Rosa and my parents were sitting next to Janice's parents, three rows back.

Once the play was underway, we stood backstage, listening to the singing. I was beginning to wish I'd been given a singing part. It would have been easier.

'Are you nervous?' said Janice.

I nodded.

Nathan came off stage, saw us standing together and made a face at me. Then Janice got into the bed that was being rolled on stage in the dark. She looked at me, smiled.

I didn't smile back. Where was being nice getting me? Nathan took the piss every time he saw me, and Janice seemed to think she was my new best friend. I kept stumbling over choices, and nothing I did felt natural any more. Low lights came up on stage. It was night time, aunt Betty was asleep. I felt a push in my back and turned. 'Get on!' hissed Boulton. I stepped on to the stage.

It was like looking down from high up; I felt dizzy and a bit sick. I stood still a moment, took a breath, and looked around. Chest of drawers to my left. I pulled open a drawer and looked through it. Nothing I did felt natural. Pulled out a necklace, and then a big pair of knickers. There was a laugh from the audience. I pocketed both, went to the dressing table and picked up a bracelet, pocketed it, then picked up a hairbrush. I was supposed to drop this, and then aunt Betty would wake. Why would a burglar drop a hairbrush? Why would he pick it up in the first place? I looked at it, and looked at Janice. She was turned away from the audience, towards me, her eyes were open and she was waiting for her cue. Beyond her, my parents and her parents and Rosa and the teachers and everyone else was watching. Behind me, Nathan and Boulton and Syd and Carly and everyone else. Choice. I decided not to drop the hairbrush. I'd just walk off the stage instead.

Janice sat up. 'Who's that? Who's there?' She fiddled with a lamp by her bed, and more light spread on to the stage. Too late to walk off.

I knocked a radiator with my knuckles. 'I'm your radiators.'

'I beg your pardon?'

Our voices sounded weak, lost in the big hall.

'Plumber. Didn't you call a plumber?'

'It's three o'clock in the morning. And my necklace appears to be hanging out of your pocket. Tell me, don't be alarmed, why are you doing this? You don't have to be a burglar.'

'What do you know about my life? Maybe burgling's all I'm good at, maybe it's what I'm best at.'

She waited, smiling at me, eyes wide and excited. Choice again. *I won't make my speech.* I wasn't even sure I could remember it if I wanted to. I was still three paces away from Janice. *I won't kiss her either.* I went for the necklace and the bracelet. I was supposed to drop them on her bed. The big knickers came out instead, getting another laugh from the audience. I laughed too, at the strangeness of standing there in front of all those people with knickers in my hand, and Janice staring at me now like she didn't know me.

Syd and Carly came on. I watched the audience while they sang their song and tied me up. With the lights still low on stage, I could just about make out Rosa smirking at me like she'd won an argument, had known best, had been right all along. So I decided—up there on stage with a hundred people as witnesses—I decided I would never be Rosa's friend, I would always remember and be faithful to this moment of hating her.

'Nice bit of business with the knickers,' said Boulton as I came off. 'We'll keep that.'

Nathan punched my arm. 'Good one. Glad it's over, eh?'

Nice is no good anyway; nice is feeble and pale and no one likes it, its hair is the colour of butterscotch and it smells of clean tissues. Hate is easy, and usually popular. Janice was coming off stage, so I slipped away. Ran down the corridor, past the changing rooms we used for make-up, into the playground and away. I was panting already, a pain developing in my chest, but I kept running. Ran home as fast as I could, as if I was trying to put distance between me and that nicer version of myself, the one who was still up there on the stage, stuck there where he'll always be, giving the unexpected speech and melting Janice's heart with a tender kiss. Why in the world would I want to be him?

1995: THERE'S A HOLE IN EVERYTHING

Had to learn one of Hamlet's I'm-so-depressed speeches last night. *Oh, that this too, too solid flesh would melt.* You do just want to slap him sometimes. In class today, remembering it and writing it down, I'm watching people's eyes glaze and their lips move as they pull words out of their brains. I wouldn't mind if my flesh melted, ran down my body in a thick lava flow, so I was sitting in a puddle of myself. What would Mr Jeffers say? He'd say, 'Rosa, go and see the nurse.' I'd have to scoop my melted flesh into a plastic bag and take it with me.

I actually love the quiet bits of lessons where everyone's working and all you can hear is the sound of pens on paper. The air seems to get thicker with the strain of people thinking, so if you put your hand up it would move more slowly. I lose three marks, all for punctuation, which I don't think is fair, but I still come top.

'Hey, Rosa.' Natalie James bends to have a word on her way out, smiling like we're best mates. 'Your fan club meets this lunchtime.' I look back at her, meeting her eyes, but I know my cheeks are red and I can't think of a word to say. She just winks at me and walks away. I sit still and let everyone go, everyone moving past me and round me like I'm a blockage in a drain.

So me and Shelley bunk off. Shelley's my best mate, and she's up for it, no hesitation. We stroll out of the gate then run down the road, sprint, my bag's thumping my hip, my shirt's tight round my shoulders, some old lady's staring at me as I run by her, but I don't care. When I leave that school I feel like a weight is being lifted off me.

Me and Shelley talk like American airheads.

'So, you'd say what? About Mick? You'd say he was hot?'

Shelley grins. 'Hot, sure.'

'But really?'

'Yeah, really, I think about him when he's not there, and everything.'

'At night you think about him?'

'Stop it. Yes.'

I laugh, and so does Shelley, long, shivery giggles. 'At night you think about him?' I say it again and we laugh again, at my syntax as much as anything. Shelley doesn't mind me using words like syntax, she likes that I'm clever.

We find another tester to squirt on our already smelly wrists and throats. Shelley sniffs, serious and wrinkling, like a connoisseur.

'Hmm,' she hums. 'Sea air, petrol notes, and a touch of banisters.'

'Polished?'

'Polished.'

Shelly chugs cider from her coke can. I pick up a lipstick, Damson Blush, glossy, waterproof, twelve-hour life, and drop it into my pocket.

'And a hint of chandeliers,' I say, but we're both laughed out, so we head for the exit.

Dad gives me his dad-smile as we're eating. His skin's getting saggy and his lips are always dry, but I like his hair, thick and short and greyish-black like an old soldier.

'What did you do today?'

Bunked off, drank two cans of cider, nicked a lipstick and a CD,

51

got thrown out of three shops, and tormented Shelley's younger sister, I don't say. I don't even say who I've been with, because ever since that thing about the dress with the sequins, my parents think Shelley is a bad influence. I say, 'Mooched around some shops, went back to someone's.'

'Buy anything?'

'A CD, a lipstick, a sandwich.'

'What more could anyone want?'

He says things like that. Thinks he's funny.

Mum looks at me, maybe a bit too casual. 'Everything OK?'

I shake my head. 'Fine.' I can suddenly sense one of those situations coming up, where I get talked at in an under-standing way. *You're not a kid, but you're not an adult either.* 'Homework,' I say, getting up.

Dad likes to have the last word. 'And, by the way, you stink.'

I give him my look, mouth twisted like granddad after his stroke, and leave him and Mum to whatever they do with themselves.

Finish my homework with the music up loud in my head-phones. It's about Hamlet and Ophelia. She beseeches him to listen to her, but he's too bothered about his own prob-lems. That makes him a jerk, in my opinion. She doesn't say beseech but I use it in my essay because it's currently my favourite word. When someone beseeches you, you have to notice, because it means they're really giving it everything. Whatever it is they want must matter more than anything else.

When my homework's done I lie on my bed with a book, not reading it, just staring at it. Then I put it down and stare out of the window at the sky. Uncle Frank used to lie on the grass with me in the park. We'd lie on our backs and watch the clouds moving and bumping into each other. I'd say *That one looks like a fat man swimming,* and he'd say *That one looks like a piano that's fallen into a tree.* He didn't try to be funny, like Dad, he just was funny. I thought so, anyway. He told me he'd once found an ear in the grass, a real human ear, and it was only much later I realised he'd got that from some film he'd seen. For a long time I looked for ears like other people look for four leaf clovers. He died, which made my mum cry for a week. I thought for a long time they might have made a mistake, that they buried someone else and he'd just turn up one day. I didn't think it exactly, but I hoped it. When I remember him, I usually think of lying on the grass beside him. He said you could feel the curve of the world beneath you, and he said if you looked at the sky long enough you felt like you could almost see the stars, even though the sun was shining. He was right about both those things.

My older brother's never home, mostly, and evenings are boring. I write my diary and then listen at my door and tip-toe out on to the landing. Voices downstairs. They've turned off the TV and for once they're talking to each other. I sit at the top of the stairs where I'm just out of sight and eaves-drop. I think I'd make an excellent spy.

Dad: 'I dreamt she was falling over, she was at the top of the stairs and she was about to fall down them and I couldn't catch her.'

Mum: 'Dreams. Dreams are over-rated.'

Dad: 'But you know what I mean.'

Mum: 'The question is what to do about it.'

Dad: 'When I was fourteen I was the same. In a few years this'll probably be just a blip.'

What to do about what? Me and Shelley talk about this

whole exchange on the phone. How parents think they know you, but they don't. How after the talk about periods you get all the lectures—cigarettes, alcohol, drugs, sex—and after that you're pretty much on your own.

Shelley goes 'They mean well,' and I'm like, 'Duh. So what? They don't even know what's happening in my life.' Mum used to be a physio before she started training in counselling. I think she should have stuck with pulled muscles.

Shelley goes 'Have you tried telling them?'

She means about Natalie James and the fan club and everything. How they hate me because I'm clever, or else because they just like having someone to hate. Of course I haven't tried. It would be too embarrassing, and if I did and they went to school to complain I think I would actually physically die of embarrassment. There'd be an autopsy, George Clooney out of E.R. would cut me open and look at my heart and push his finger around in my guts and he'd take off his mask and point those big brown eyes at Mum and Dad, all sad and softly spoken but accusing. 'You should never have put her through it,' he'd say. 'This girl died for nothing.' Or, no, 'This beautiful girl died for nothing.' My mum would be crying, Dad would be looking at his shoes, and George Clooney would be literally holding my heart in his hands.

'You thought you knew her,' George would say, 'but you didn't.'

Me and Shelley can talk about stuff like that. She doesn't think it's weird that my George Clooney fantasy has him doing an autopsy on me.

Natalie sits on her desk staring at me. History is always worst, because Miss Hinde is always late. There could be ten minutes of this.

54

'So, Rosa, how's things?'

Gravity is on Natalie's side, people are drawn to her, their heads all turn towards her. Even mine does. Me and Shelley read *Company* in a shop and it said visualise your personality. I visualised Natalie's. It's a great big wave that grabs other people and sucks them in and pulls them along in her direction. You almost can't blame her for enjoying the power she has. I think she knows it might not last and she's making the most of it. It's just some lucky mix of people, circumstances and her nasty streak all combining to make her the one everyone looks to. She came up with the WE LOVE ROSA badges, and began the campaign about my so-called body odour. Stealing my things—a hair-slide, a biro—that was Natalie's idea too.

'Who's Shelley?'

I keep ignoring her, but I start to bite the inside of my mouth. She picks up a book and shows it to me. It's my diary. She flicks through it.

'Me and Shelley, me and Shelley, me and Shelley.'

This is very bad.

'Who'd be sad and stupid enough to be your friend?'

Please God, let Miss Hinde come in now.

'Know what I think?'

Yes, I do know, but I don't want to hear it.

'I think Shelley's your imaginary friend. It says she lives on Bywell Street, and Suzie lives there and she doesn't know a Shelley. Is that true, Rosa?' She sounds almost caring. 'Is she your made-up friend?'

I get up, slow and controlled, put my History books in my bag and take my diary from her. She doesn't stop me. Then I walk out of the class. No one's laughing. It feels like it's gone beyond laughing. Natalie says goodbye.

No one tries to stop me as I walk down the corridors and

out of the door. I've noticed that—if you look like you know where you're going and what you're doing, people tend not to question you.

Uncle Frank got depressed before he died. One of the things he said was 'Afternoons are hideous, Rosa, hideous. You've lost your energy from the morning, and you haven't got your evening vibe going.' That's what he said. I never really get an evening vibe going, but as I walk out of school I know what he meant about afternoons.

The time is what he called the drifting middle of the day. The road's empty, but I can hear the thrum of traffic, the whine of brakes, like whale song, the wheezing of exhausts. I keep walking, slow and calm, listening to the air move in the trees. A TV is flickering behind a window. Uncle Frank said if you were quiet enough yourself, you could hear everything. I hear a baby crying, and a dog barking and scrabbling at a door. The sun, behind a cloud but near to the edge of it, makes the light dramatic, makes me feel like I'm in a film. I get that sometimes, the feeling that I'm up above my left shoulder, looking at me. Sometimes everyone else is looking at me at the same time and I'm like them, I'm thinking *What's wrong with her? She's pathetic, why doesn't she fight back or something?* Other times it's like now, I'm alone and I see this girl just walking down the road and I feel a bit sorry for her. I wish things could go better for her. I don't know if it happens to everyone or if it means I'm going mad.

Things I want:

One: I want Natalie James to die or have a disfiguring accident or have to move to Iran because of her dad's work and wear an all-over veil.

Two: I want someone to use the word *beseech*. And it wouldn't sound stupid, it would be exactly the right word.

It would be best if it was a boy using it, talking to me, but even if it wasn't I'd like to hear it, I'd like people to speak like that and mean it.

Three: I want nothing else bad to happen.

I'm on my back in the grass. As far as I can see, the whole park is empty, everyone is somewhere else. Uncle Frank said if someone on another planet was looking at our planet, we wouldn't be lying under the sky, we'd be part of the sky. I like that. Part of someone else's sky. I pull up a blade of grass with my fingers, scrunch it up and smell it. I'm trying to feel the curve of the whole world under my back, but I can't, it's just the park. School's a mile in one direction, home's a mile in the other, and I'm stuck between the two. And of the two people I care most about, Frank's dead and Shelley's gone missing.

I turn my head and there she is.

'Kill Natalie,' she says. 'Just kill her. Kill her. Seriously.'

Me and Shelley met at primary school. We promised to be best friends for ever. Pinpricks in palms, hands squashed together to mix our blood. Hamlet was wrong, you think you're solid, but actually you're not. Look closely enough, look at the back of your hand, smooth and creamy as custard, you'll see you're full of holes. I like that, because it means I might still have a little bit of Shelley in my veins and she might, wherever she is, have a bit of Rosa pumping round her body. That's the way it is with real friends, you're part of each other. She moved away with her family after she'd been there for a term and a half. We managed a couple of letters, that was all. I've never seen her again. She's not an imaginary friend though, she's a might-have-been friend, a should-have-been friend.

'Follow her into the toilets. Your mum's letter-opener in

the throat, from behind. Wash your hands and walk away. Kill the bitch.'

My duvet smells biscuity, my *Hamlet* smells of clean pages, I've got sensuous essential oils burning. All this should be calming and restful. *Oh, that this too, too solid flesh would melt.* I should be feeling OK now.

There's a knock. 'Can I come in, Rosa?'

Mum's got her hand in her hair. It's curly and dark same as mine, only longer. Her nose is bigger than mine and she's got a whole flock of crows' feet. I know she's upset about something because she's used my name, because of the hand in the hair and because her eyes have gone small. She sits on my orange beanbag with the big brown flowers on it, her knees higher than her shoulders. It's from the seventies and it belonged to Dad and I refuse to throw it away. She shifts beans with her bum.

'So.' Her eyes move over my school shirt on the floor, the sticky plate on the desk, my tipped-over bag, my Take That poster. 'Heard you disappeared in the middle of school today?'

I shrug.

'Miss Hinde says it's happened before, and lately she says you've seemed quiet. Preoccupied?'

Uncle Frank once said that the first big surprise about your parents is that they don't know everything, and the second big surprise is they're not as stupid as you think. He was definitely my favourite relative, but he would go on a bit sometimes even before he got depressed, and you'd get the feeling he really liked listening to himself. On the night that it happened he rang up my mum and wanted to talk to her. She was busy so he asked her to put me on. She looked at me, I remember, eyebrows raised, and I nodded and took the phone. He seemed just the same as he'd been recently, going on, listening to himself, not completely making sense. Eventually we said bye and apparently he drove off in his car and did it not much later.

Mum stayed in bed for a week, but we had a long chat, her in the bed, me sitting on it. She told me, with her eyes all baggy and red, that neither of us could have made any difference, that Uncle Frank had made a decision, a selfish one and a wrong one and a sad one, and we shouldn't feel guilty about it. I think she's right. What he didn't do was beseech me or her to listen to him. He was more Hamlet than Ophelia, all shouty and intense and actually a bit scary.

Mum's doing her quiet thing, waiting for me to say something.

'Ever wanted to kill anyone?'

This makes her go all thoughtful. 'Yes, actually,' she says. 'A man named Dan.' At a different time this might be interesting, but right now I don't want reminiscences, so I start again.

'What would you do if I murdered someone?'

'I think I'd still love you. You planning to?'

'Not sure,' I say.

For some reason this reassures her. She sinks lower in the beanbag. She looks really uncomfortable.

'If I wanted to change schools, could I?'

'Maybe. You going to tell me what's up?'

I've been reading Sylvia Plath and Virginia Woolf, leaving them lying around sort of as a hint. *Hello? I'm not very happy.* Mum doesn't like hints, she likes things out in the open. That's her counselling.

'Say you beseech me.'

'What?'

'Seriously. Without being sarcastic or anything. Please?'
She's sitting there staring at me with her knees near her ears, probably wondering what drugs I'm on.
'Rosa, I beseech you to tell me what's wrong.'
So I do.

1999: THE PRETTY HORSE

THE INTERVIEW TOOK place in Mr Scott's office on Friday afternoon. He sat straight-backed behind his desk, face lowered and partly hidden behind his hands. His finger-muffled words sniped out after a silence of several seconds.

'You don't like telesales, do you?'

Sean resisted the temptation to shrug. 'I do it well enough.'

Mr Scott lowered his hands, smiled wetly, and shuffled a couple of stapled pages from the mess in front of him. 'You've failed to fill in your weekly self-assessments, your supervisor has graded you low-to-average, and you've been late three times so far this month. It's not what we expect at Newman's. Comments?'

Sean looked thoughtful. 'Sorry?' he suggested.

Mr Scott sighed. 'This is a final warning, Sean. If you're late again, you're out. Can you afford to be without a job?'

'No.' Sean nodded. 'Not really.'

'Think on that over the weekend.' Mr Scott leaned forward, across his desk. 'Sean, I like you. You're not thick, you're bright. You're not thick, Sean. You could enjoy this.' He pointed a finger, like a gun. 'Smile while you're on the telephone,' the gun hand opened and tilted between himself and Sean, 'engage the customer in a cosy, mutual interaction. Don't think of it as sales, think of it as a little dance.' His inclining shoulders quivered in illustration. 'Do you understand?'

Mr Scott straightened his spine again. Sean said 'Yes.' Mr Scott said 'Goodbye. Thank you.'

Sean stood and shook his head. 'No, thank *you*.'

Saturday. Sean was standing on one leg in the park. He raised his left knee up towards his chest, slowly, as if some broad, resisting current in the air was moving against him. One hand, palm outwards, slid across his body, the other, partly curled, reached into space. He stood first on one leg, then on the other, pointing his toes like a gymnast on a bar. Only his face was still. Experience, and the films of Bruce Lee, had told him that changing his expression in slow motion looked ridiculous.

The breeze stirred around him, and sunlight moved over his skin. Old people sat on benches, a man walked a vicious dog, kids kicked a ball around. He was unaware. He was moving at the world's pace. If he could jump in this sluggish style he would land on a different spot, as the earth turned beneath him.

He practised Tai Chi regularly. On a good day it appeared to heighten his senses, making him feel both alert and serene. He also hoped, so far without evidence, that it might be a way of meeting girls. He stood in his baggy shorts and grey T-shirt, and appeared to conduct the symphony of the park. The birds and the dog walkers, the drunks and addicts, all glanced or stared at him, and the magisterial sweep of his hand seemed to acknowledge and dismiss them. Only he was in tune with the slow, tectonic shift of ageing in which they were all engaged.

'You look like a prat.' It was Cole. 'We going, or what?'

Sean put both feet down on the ground. 'Yeah, let's go.'

Cole's studio was a bare, echoey room with high, arched

windows and peeling lino on the floor. It felt like a disused church, and Sean's spirits always sank as he entered. He spent most Saturdays there. He was meant to be Cole's assistant, but really he was just company. Sean put the radio on, took two beers out of the fridge, then sat down to watch Cole welding half a pushchair to half a shopping trolley.

'Critique on consumer culture,' said Cole.

'I'm on the verge of losing my job,' said Sean.

'So what, it's a crap job.'

Sean found himself irritated, perhaps because he knew Cole was right. 'Can I just say, there's a fine line between artistic activity and a complete waste of time.'

'There's a fine line,' said Cole, 'between almost anything and a complete waste of time.'

Then Cole told him that looking like a lame mime artist in the park didn't seem very constructive. Sean told him Tai Chi was an ancient martial art, and maybe he should get out more. Cole said Sean was wasting his life, Sean said he should talk.

Cole pulled goggles over his eyes, and a small triangular flame fizzed out of his torch. Sean sat back and watched. The truth was, he envied Cole, because Cole had always known what he wanted to do. It was thanks to him that Sean had got his art A level. Cole had looked over Sean's shoulder at his broad red stripes of paint, with little, crudely drawn men squashed between them.

'What's this?' he said. 'Rothko meets Lowry?'

'Who?' said Sean.

'Don't know what you're doing, do you?'

Sean didn't know what he was doing. He was just daubing something vaguely decorative on the paper. Cole showed Sean his portfolio, sifting through the paint-stiff paper. Sean smelt the sweet, faintly tarry oils emerging from the leaves. 'Have this one,' said Cole. Sean just stared at him. 'Have it.' Sean wasn't sure if he was serious. 'Go on, you'll never pass with what you're doing.' Sean laughed. So did Cole.

Manchester United one, Tottenham Hotspur . . .

The announcer's voice rose an octave, as if he was surprised.

. . . three.

Cole had turned off the torch. Now he was holding half a baby, trying to decide how to attach it to half a bag of shopping.

'What's your problem?' he said. 'Your parents?'

Sean looked non-committal.

'All right, suppose this, suppose they got squashed by a falling tree. OK? They're dead. Are you happy or sad?'

Sean paused.

'No pausing, straight off: happy or sad?'

'I'm not happy.'

'You're sad?'

'I guess. But I'm not heartbroken.'

God knows what he felt about his parents. God knows what they felt about him. Sean felt that he hardly featured in their lives any more. They'd given up nagging him. Any pressure they exerted was all done with looks and sighs, except half the time they were looking and sighing at each other. He felt he didn't much feature in anyone's life any more, except Cole's. They naturally gravitated together. Cole said he was rejecting the outmoded structures and values of art college, Sean said he was taking a break after disappointing A level results. It felt like there was an unspoken agreement between them: each relied on the other to fail. For Cole to have a successful exhibition, or for Sean to

suddenly leave town, or for either of them to enter a serious, long-term relationship, would have been an almost
unthinkable selfishness.

'What's *your* problem, Cole? Have you even got one?'

Cole didn't answer for a moment, filling his bisected
Safeways bag. Fish fingers. Soap wrapped in cellophane.
Then he looked at Sean. 'You really want to know?'

'Sure.'

'My problem is, I'm not sure, not a hundred per cent,
whether I'm gay or straight.'

Now Sean was silent. That was the thing about Cole, it
was one of the things about him. You didn't know if he was
serious or not.

'Course you're sure.'

'I'm not.'

'OK, answer straight away, don't pause. Ready?'

'Go on.'

'Who do you fancy, me or Rosa?'

'You.'

'You don't.'

'I do,' said Cole. 'Actually I quite fancy your sister too,
since you're asking.'

'Well that's not going to happen. You do know that,
don't you?'

'Which, you or your sister?'

'Neither. But definitely not me.'

'So you're saying your sister's up for a shag?'

'No.'

Cole put a variety pack of cereals into the bag. It fell out.
'Anyway,' he said, 'I've got the answer to your problem. My
place has a spare room. Move in.'

Sean was used to not having much to think about. He
was having trouble registering all this.

'You know I'm straight?'

Cole grinned at him. 'I'm just hoping Rosa is.'

That was Saturday. He spent half of Sunday in bed. Half-man, half-duvet, his mother called him. She didn't get it. Sean felt as if he was holding something; it was not heavy, but it was big and awkwardly shaped. He didn't know why he had to hold it but he did, he had to carry it, shifting it from arm to arm, on to his shoulder, on to his back.

He'd had careers advice. He'd filled out an aptitude test. *What is your favourite colour? What did you dream about last night? Why is grass green?*

'Avoid working with the public,' the woman had said. 'Your affiliation skills are poor.' She was wearing a thin cotton top. He could see her bra through it, although he was trying not to. 'The worst job in the world for you would be telephone sales.' He hadn't worked out yet whether women knew when you were looking at their breasts. Even if he focused on her chin he could make out the embroidered lace edging. 'Your maths is good and you like art. Have you thought about design? How about architecture?'

He could see himself poring over a blueprint, pointing out a flaw. Striding around a building site, wearing a hard hat. Keeping his contact with the public to a minimum. He'd be known as terse. *That's Sean Dax over there. Don't worry about his manner, he's just terse. Yes, him in the yellow hat.*

That was Sunday morning. Just before lunch the scene diverged from his memory of it a little, when the careers officer took her top off. They affiliated.

Sunday afternoon, whatever room he went into, apart from his own, he ran into family. His father cooking something, his mother reading the paper, Rosa in his father's office, in one of her chat rooms. He looked in on each, bored by himself, then came back to Rosa and sat on the floor while she typed.

She ignored him. He looked at scripts stacked on shelves, piles of videos, stacks of waste paper ready for reuse. The computer whined. She was still ignoring him.

'I might leave,' he said. 'I might move in with Cole.'

Her fingers chattered over the keys as she spoke. 'Thought you wanted to move to London?'

'I did. I do.'

'Newsflash, Sean—Cole doesn't live in London. He lives round the corner.'

He wanted to be in north London, near a tube, studying something unusual at college, working nights in a poky little bar, sleeping with a girl with short dark hair and surprising piercings.

'Cole's place would be a start.'

She turned away from the screen and looked at him. 'Nothing's ever definite with you.'

'Can you see me as an architect?'

'It's the rest of your life, Sean. Stop arsing about and make a decision.'

'Arsing about?' He laughed, she kicked him. 'Say hello to your invisible friends,' he said, as he left.

Monday morning. The sky was white, the streets were quiet. Sean threaded the truanting footballers, passed by the old people, gave the dogs their due berth, with every step making banal but crucial decisions about timing and trajectory. He took a left, not a right, so he went around the bandstand, and so he saw the horse.

Saddled but riderless, it was nuzzling among peonies,

occasionally stamping the ground impatiently. It didn't move as Sean approached, it had discovered something blue that it liked the taste of, and it didn't notice him.

Sean touched the smooth, gleaming flank, and the horse shook its hindquarters irritably, so he tried again, with a firm pat. The horse didn't react. He pushed his face into its side and inhaled. Straw, shit, soap. There was a number on a metal plate on the saddle. wpc579. A truncheon stuck rudely out of a pouch. Was the horse under a spell? If he kissed it, might it turn into a beautiful policewoman? He moved round slowly in front of it, stroking its long muzzle, holding the bridle lightly, looking into its bulging eyes. It had long teeth, like alien's teeth, behind drawn back, curled-up lips. He got as close as he dared to their fleshy, wet undersides, pale pink and quivering. A kiss was out of the question.

There was a notion floating in Sean's mind that you were supposed to breathe into a horse's nose, to gain its trust. He looked around, but saw no one. No policewoman emerging embarrassed from public toilets, no handler skiving briefly to play football. Just the kids, old people, dogs. The horse was looking at him now, apparently having had enough to eat, so he leant forward, towards the indecent nostrils, wide, black holes in its muzzle. He pursed his lips and puffed some air up the left one. The horse yanked its head back, snorted, and looked more carefully at Sean, as if wondering what his game was.

'Sorry,' said Sean. 'Bit forward, sorry.'

It seemed to be reassured by his low, steady voice. Sean would have liked to climb on. He'd never ridden a horse before and he liked to experience something new every week or so. Lately, it had been difficult. The last new thing he'd experienced was an unusual flavour of yoghurt from

Kwik Save. He would have liked to try this, to make himself comfortable in the narrow slope of the saddle, to thigh-squeeze those heavy-breathing sides, and see where the creature took him. He had to get to Newman's on time though, in order to keep his job. And the the horse scared him a little. Its solid, unknowable presence was unnerving.

The police station was almost on his way. He would lead the horse, and leave it at the desk. He still had time.

It was willing to follow. In fact it shoved its head over his shoulder and nuzzled his cheek, then walked ahead of him, pulling him along. When he tried to run ahead it started to run too, or trot, a bouncy, frisky stride, as if it was engaged in a game with its new friend. It was a horse at some unusual pitch of horse-exuberance, a horse taking time-out from its usual existence, a horse on holiday. Sean, jogging and puffing alongside it, found it poignant. Why was he less happy than a horse?

By the time he reached the police station he was exhausted. It was shut. It was open all day Saturday, and four mornings a week. Due to budgetary requirements it was closed Mondays.

Hard to know what to do. He wanted a coffee and his favourite cafe was in the shopping centre, which was also the quickest way to work. But could he take the horse into the centre? Avoiding the centre would mean there was no time to stop. Coffee, horse, horse, coffee. *Nothing's ever definite with you.*

He tried to look casual. He backed through the double-doors, pulling the horse after him, then he led it by the reins, not bothering to look behind, like a man with a small dog on a lead. He tried to feel casual. Tried to imagine understanding the horse on some deep, animal level, talking to it and gaining its trust, like one of those dour boys in a Cormac McCarthy novel, where man and rider are in harmony with each other and with the earth and the sky. Difficult. There was no sky in the shopping centre, except quartered in the glass-panelled roof above the fountain and novelty clock, and no earth either, just shops, half of them closed, and the flat, grey tiles of the long corridor.

By now he'd registered everything Cole had said to him. He still hadn't decided what to do about it, but he'd registered it. Leaving home to live with Cole might be good, but if he stayed at home, and managed to keep his job, he'd be able to save more money. Or was that just prevarication? He'd been mulling it over, and he'd hoped that Monday morning would bring a new clarity to his thinking. He hadn't counted on the horse though. Its hooves echoed like the ticking of a grandfather clock.

It was tempting to keep it, but not practical. His record with pets was not good. He'd had a hamster once that had bitten off its own leg, and a goldfish that had exploded when he overfed it. The family had discussed having a dog, but had decided against it. No one could guarantee that they'd walk it regularly. No one could even guarantee that they'd feed it regularly. He'd fed a friend's cat for a week once, and the smell of cheap meat in the mornings had nearly made him throw up.

He sat at a flimsy table with an expresso in one hand and the contents of three sugar sachets in the other. The horse licked the crystals from his palm, rough-tongued. Everyone inside the cafe was watching him. He tried to look casual again.

What would be good now would be to put a tent in some sort of horse rucksack and set out somewhere, put some distance between him and everything else. He could visit Edinburgh, Manchester, Southampton, all the places his friends were. *Yeah, I was getting a bit bored, so I bought a horse. What do you think?* Nice idea, but it was still hard to imagine getting on the horse, taking control of it.

'Hey mate, is he yours?'

Sean put down his miniature coffee cup. 'I'm looking after him.'

'I ride horses, let me have a go.'

He was a couple of years younger than Sean, seventeen, eighteen, but he was a big bloke with a sneer and hard eyes. 'Go on, give us a go.' He had his hands on the saddle, his foot going for the stirrup.

'Get off.'

Sean was suddenly standing, shoulders tensing, his breath audible. He was suddenly angry and ready for, almost eager for a fight. The bloke had paused, reading the metal plate on the saddle.

'Are you a copper?'

Sean didn't answer.

'You look like a fucking WPC.'

Sean just stared, glared, waited.

He'd never been brave before. He got into a fight by accident years ago, at school, when he'd been taking the piss out of Paul McCarthy in, he thought, a friendly way. Suddenly Paul was pushing him in the chest, swearing at him, saying he was sick of him, and when Sean tried to deflect his hand, only to stop the pushing, he swung a punch. Sean barely defended himself, he was too surprised, he got hit in the side of the head, then in the stomach, and then in the face. Paul stopped when he saw blood flowing out of Sean's nose, said 'Watch yourself,' and walked away. Sean was like, *What just happened?* Clutching his face, tasting his blood, swallowing it.

Now he was furious, too angry to be scared. Who was

this kid, messing with his horse? They held each other's gaze for several seconds, then the bloke backed off, laughed and shook his head like it was nothing to him, and walked away. Confidence, Sean knew, was the key. Confidence was the key to picking up girls and, apparently, it was the key to scaring off thugs. Sean took the horse's reins again, and headed for the way out of the shopping centre. It was twenty past nine. If he didn't get to work in ten minutes, he was going to lose his job.

When he emerged from the centre, he saw the bloke waiting for him. He headed towards Newman's, leading the horse, wondering what to do, the bloke trailing along behind him. Sean was praying for inspiration. He couldn't see Mr Scott welcoming the horse into the office. He led it down the High Street, turned right past Smiths. He dawdled, looked back over his shoulder. Abruptly, suspiciously, he was alone.

Sean paused, felt the grainy texture of the wall beside him. Flattened his hand against it, as if it was in danger of toppling over on to him. He was breathing hard. He had a feeling that if he looked up at the sky he might feel dizzy.

Without premeditation, he raised his leg, put his foot in the horse's stirrup, and hoisted himself up. He almost went over the other side, but adjusted his balance and sat there, cautious, his spine rigid. It was unexpectedly high. Surprising, what a thrill it was. The horse stirred, uneasy, so he gently poked his heels into its side. Nothing. He jabbed, feeling a little give in the bouncy, tight-swollen flanks, and suddenly he was moving, he wasn't labouring any more, pulling the horse or being pulled by it, he was tenuously, scarily in tune with it. This was better than slow-motion Tai Chi, better than anything his weekend had offered. It was a jolting movement, it seemed uneven at first, and never less than precarious, but there was definitely something exhilarating about it. Maybe this was what being brave felt like.

A hundred yards on, he was in a quiet backstreet, approaching the office. He dismounted reluctantly and leant his face against the saddle, the horse standing still and patient. Took a deep breath, still not knowing what he was going to do. He smelt leather and the straw-shit-soap cocktail.

When he lifted his head he saw the bloke for the third time, now with two of his mates. Sean froze, beside the horse, and they stared at each other, like gunfighters. One against three, like in *High Noon*. Confidence is the key, except when running away is the key. Now, clearly, was the time to vault back on to the horse in one fluid movement, dig his heels into its sides and gallop away, down this backstreet, back on to the High Street, then the Inner Distribution Road, and then right out of town, somewhere beyond. London perhaps, and a new life free of Mr Scott, and thugs, his sighing parents and his sarcastic sister, the complications presented by his best friend, his disappointing A levels and his indefinite break, and the invisible, awkwardly shaped burden that he was now carrying again, had been carrying from the moment his foot touched the pavement as he got down from the horse.

But the three blokes were walking backwards. One of them pointed, shouted something irrelevant, then they were all round a corner and gone, back into their own lives, out of his.

'Where'd you find him, son?'

He didn't even have time to be puzzled. He turned to see the policewoman as she took the reins out of his hands.

'The park. The police station was closed.'

73

She smiled, looked into his eyes for three seconds, then led the horse away. He nodded. He had less than a minute left before he lost his job, and the momentum of the moment—thugs one way, policewoman the other—was pushing him towards the office. He hesitated in the dangling seconds, watching the long, fragile legs of the horse. It was a few steps ahead of its new minder, its hooves tapping out a jaunty rhythm. It was back in safe hands and knew where it was going. Sean hesitated a moment longer, then followed it, flexing his shoulders like a walker with a heavy rucksack, making it tolerably comfortable before he sets off.

1999: THE REALM OF THE POSSIBLE

WHAT ARE BROTHERS for? a) He's never here. b) When he is here I wish he wasn't. c) I can't stand the way he eats apples. d) Or drinks coffee. He sort of sucks it in and makes a lip-smacking noise. I don't even know if it's just to annoy me or if it's really how he drinks coffee, like it's a disability or something. e) My friends fancy him. Why do they? I've told them about the apples and the coffee, also about the snide remarks, also about the fact that there are definitely times when he smells. Why would anybody fancy him?

I was reading about Queen Elizabeth's parliaments, wondering why I chose History when I could have done another language, or I could have done Maths and surprised everybody. The Long Parliament. They were all long, weren't they? And what does *prorogued* mean? The door opened and Sean came in. No knock, obviously. He walked in and suddenly my room felt cramped. He's too tall, Sean, that's probably where he gets his arrogance from. Tall and thin, with spikey hair. I'd call him gawky.

'Why are you so good at school? Why aren't you having any fun?' He sat down and stretched his legs out, crossed at the ankle, like he was settling in for a while. 'Seriously,' he said.

He does this when he's bored, which is often these days. He comes in and tries to wind me up. 'You know when you do Tai Chi?' I said. 'You look like an idiot. I can't believe you do that in public.'

He nodded thoughtfully, like this was the answer he'd

expected. 'I think you're scared of life. Is that right?'

I didn't say anything, just gave him my withering look. He was wrong as it happened, because I'd made a definite decision to cultivate spontaneity, but I wasn't going to tell him that because he'd only take the piss. And I could tell he was already enjoying this. He always enjoyed our arguments, as long as they remained simply abusive. It was when they became more specific that they got hurtful or demoralising. Perhaps that's why he abruptly changed the subject. He told me something I guessed he'd been saving up, about his mate Cole.

'Cole said the same thing about Tai Chi a while ago. Said I looked like a mime artist with a limp. And I'll tell you something else he said: I go, *Who do you fancy, me or Rosa?* and he said me. He said you as well, but he said me. I had to make it clear what sexuality I'm not.'

Now my mind moved right off the Long Parliament. 'Cole said he fancied me?'

'You're missing the point. He said he fancied me.'

I said I thought we were probably all bisexual if environmental and cultural taboos were removed, look what went on in prisons. Sean said speak for yourself.

As soon as he was gone, I was in front of the mirror. Am I pleased a bisexual man fancies me, or does it just mean I look like a boy? My eyes looked at themselves. Ordinary hazel. I saw doubt, no guile, but a pinch of unattractive need. Is that what a boy sees? Probably not. Partly because I don't really do eye-contact, partly because boys look at other things. Hair, skin, tits, lips, make-up. All of which were there and sort of OK, except the make-up, because I don't really do make-up either. How did I feel about Cole fancying me? I was pleased. I'm basically pleased if anyone fancies me.

I went across the landing to Sean's room, and knocked.
I always knock, because I'm a bit worried about what I
might find if I don't. I waited a second, then entered. Sean
was lying on his bed, he had a hand on the window and he
was drumming the glass like a convict passing the time.

'Anyway, I'm going to a party tomorrow,' I said. 'So, what
do you know?' I left again before he could answer.

Jackie's party. Since I moved schools I'm not exactly Miss
Popularity, but no one seems to hate me either. Jackie's one
of those brown haired, big-eyed girls who only expect to
meet nice people and have nice things happen to them, and
who are mostly not disappointed. She sat next to me in
French and said she wished she was as clever as me. She
said she liked my hair. She nodded towards Andy Butter
and said something about his name. I didn't catch it, but I
laughed anyway. She probably invited me to her party
because she thinks of herself as a good person.

Things I want.

One: To go to Jackie's party and have two or three people smile and say *There's Rosa*, and one of them immediately
come up and start a conversation, so there's none of that
trying to look as if you like standing on your own, or trying
to look relaxed on the edge of other people's conversations.

Two: An older sister instead of an older brother.

Three: To have sex with Andy Butter.

I hadn't expected to write that third one in my diary, but
there it was. I was sitting at my desk looking out of the window at the bare silhouettes of the trees against the sky,
listening to Sean's music whining next door, and then I
looked down at the page and wrote *Three: To have sex with
Andy Butter*. Spontaneously.

Sean's music stopped and I heard him going down the

77

stairs. I followed. I didn't know why, *But that's good*, I told myself, *not knowing why is good*. I stood on the stairs and watched him lean into the sitting room.

'Going out,' he said. 'Drink with Cole.'

All I heard in reply was the theme tune of Dad's soap, *Calder's Road*, then he was gone. If Dad was watching TV, Mum was probably somewhere else, in their bedroom or the kitchen. They don't tend to spend much time together. So I just walked out. Bottom of the stairs, one, two, three steps to the front door, soft hands on the latch, and I was gone too.

Cold air hit me. I was wearing a thin top and I hadn't picked up a coat. But it felt feeble to slip back indoors, so I kept going. Some girls on their way to a club on a winter's night wear hardly anything. You see them clacking down the street with their skinny arms crossed and their breath making clouds. Not me. First of all I don't go to clubs, and second if I did I'd wear something warm.

Now that I was outside, following Sean felt a bit feeble too. Did I need to borrow his life to make mine more interesting? So I went in the same direction as him, and stayed out of his sight, but decided I wasn't following him, I was heading for the park. *Don't go in the park on your own at night.* This was one of the laws I grew up with. I used to imagine there were nocturnal monsters there, living in tree trunks or underground caverns. Now I had a better idea of what kind of monsters to fear, but for the sake of spontaneity I felt I had to go anyway.

I was remembering something, shivering and hugging myself, trying to ignore my nerves, I was remembering something as I approached the park.

'We'll strike through here.'

Thick bushes overlapped each other, but Frank waded

through anyway, took my hand and pulled me after him, said 'Come on, Sean,' without bothering to look back. I looked back. Sean shrugged at me and struggled through after me, and we were off the path. Brambles, damp leaves, whipping twigs and low, sagging branches. We'd find a narrow way through, then meet an obstruction, and Frank would strike through again to some other glimpsed trail. 'Desire paths,' he said. 'You won't find them on any maps, but they'll take you where you want to go.' Things slip. First it's amusing, then it's irritating, then it's scary. You could vanish. I was six, Sean eight, and uncle Frank was some unspecific adult age. He'd taken us for a walk around Hardcastle Crags. As far as I was concerned, you could vanish in this forest. We paused. We gave up, it seemed to me, and sat down in a patch of earth, scratched and bruised and weary. I could smell something rotting. I leant on the rough bark of a tree trunk, fully believing that I would never emerge again, that the world elsewhere would continue without me, that my parents would mourn for a while but get over it, and have new children to replace me and Sean.

'You see?' said Frank. 'You see? You look for desire paths, you get lost in the woods.' It was as if we were having an argument and he was proving a point. 'All I can say for sure,' he said, 'is we're still somewhere in the realm of the possible.' We looked puzzled. 'That's where we live,' he said, 'cheek by jowl with disappointment and disquiet.'

That's when I realised he was enjoying himself, and I wasn't in the hands of a capable, reassuring adult. I looked at Sean, leaning next to me, panting slightly. He did something surprising. He held my hand in his. Squeezed it. I felt his blood move in the soft web of skin between his thumb and his index finger.

Don't go in the park on your own at night. The grass spread out in front of me, neat and unthreatening as a table cloth. What's the big deal? It's just grass. The trees up ahead swayed in the light breeze that was making me shiver. I was cold and nervous and wondering what I was doing. I'd just walk as far as the trees and then go home. After all, when I was six it turned out all right in the end.

Figures in the darkness. Suddenly I was less interested in the shape of the trees and the smell of the grass. Two figures, bulky, male. Male shapes, broad in the shoulder and speaking in male voices, walking in a male way, heavy and deliberate and like they belong, two male figures walking out of the dark line of the trees. I stopped like I'd just thought of something, I paused and looked at my watch, feeling stupid, then turned and walked back the way I'd come, towards the road and the street lights, not too fast but not too slow either, wondering what the male figures were doing behind me. Towards the road, towards the road which seemed further away than it should, like when you swim too far out and the shore never seems to get any closer as you swim back.

The male voices were close behind me. Deep, gruff sounds. I was scared now, but I could see someone on the road ahead, so I started to run, listening, trying to hear their foot-falls on the new-mown grass behind me. As long as it's not a friend of theirs I should be all right, I'm just pretending it's someone I recognise, and I'm running towards him.

It was someone I recognised.

'Sean! Sean!'

He turned. I saw his face adjusting to my presence, to the note of fear in my voice.

'What's up?'

'Nothing, nothing, I just saw you.'

He looked past me, at the two blokes who were now

coming out of the park. A middle-aged man and his weedy son.

The father said, 'Evening.' Sean nodded.

I looked at their departing backs, Sean looked at me. 'You were scared of them?'

'I thought you were going to see Cole?'

'He wasn't in. Come on.'

So we headed home, and I didn't know whether to feel embarrassed or relieved.

I pulled a sweater over my thin top and made coffee for us both. Mum came in and asked me how Elizabeth's parliaments were going. I said fine. She looked at Sean but said nothing to him, and left. They'd obviously had an argument, but since I was feeling warm to him at the moment I didn't ask, just put the two mugs on the table and sat down.

'You could come to the party if you like.'

My spontaneity project wasn't going that well, but I was persevering. I'd had no particular intention to invite him, but the thought had arrived in my head so I'd said it. He didn't answer, I wasn't sure he'd heard.

'So, you and Cole,' I tried. ' Are you going to move in with him?'

'No.'

I kept my tone bright and casual. 'What are you going to do?'

'Don't worry about it. Don't worry about me.'

A silence. Sometimes it was hard to feel warm towards Sean. 'Anyway,' I said, still bright, 'I want to show you something.'

'What?'

'How to drink coffee without making a noise. Or tea. It works with tea too.'

'Go on, then.'

I lifted my mug and quietly sipped my coffee. He watched, nodding. Then he said, 'Rosa, are you *very* unhappy?'

I laughed. 'Don't be horrible.'

'That's what we're best at though, being horrible to each other.'

A little alarm was going off in my head. Maybe he was in a bad mood because he wanted to be having a drink with Cole, or because something had happened between him and Mum, but he was still smiling, and so was I.

'But we're brother and sister,' I said. 'That means no matter how much we fall out we have to still love each other. That's how it works.'

'And you learnt that where?'

We weren't smiling any more. 'That's how it works,' I insisted. 'Because, for a start, I bet Mum and Dad are going to split up, so we should have each other.'

'When I was about nine, I decided I'd never be your friend.'

'What?'

'Because you were getting all the attention, they were suddenly realising how clever you were, and I felt left out.' He was looking at the wall and focusing on something beyond it, remembering. 'You did something . . . Anyway, you were generally getting on my nerves. I promised myself I wouldn't forgive you, I decided I'd never be your friend.'

He saw my face. 'Stupid, I know. Don't worry, I was only nine.'

'But you never have,' I said. 'You never have been my friend.'

Went to the party. Didn't hang around trying to pretend I

liked standing on my own, and didn't try to look relaxed on the edge of other people's conversations. Instead I grabbed a can of cider in the kitchen, marched up to a knot of people—Jackie, Ella, Andy Butter and another boy I didn't recognise—waited for Moby to go quiet for a moment and announced 'This cider's sweet.' Everyone looked at me. I'd spent half an hour in front of the mirror putting a face on, and then another ten minutes practising expressions. Spontaneity will only get you so far—sometimes, like a good General, or a Boy Scout, you need to prepare.

I gave them *She knows she's sexy.*

I looked Andy Butter straight in the eye. 'Do you like sweet cider?' He showed me his bottle of Stella. 'I don't get lager,' I said. 'It's bitter, isn't it?' He had floppy dark hair and small eyes, which at the moment were crinkled as if he was looking into the sun. He shrugged, but he'd moved half a step from the group, I'd succeeded in separating him, so I gave him a full blast of *I fancy you,* and said 'Can I try yours?' Crinkly eyes and no expression. Jackie, Ella and irrelevant boy watching. Time not passing, like a drip hanging from a tap, but not dripping. Then he smiled. Andy Butter smiled at me and offered me the bottle. He smiled and I took the bottle and if this was still the realm of the possible then it was good enough for me.

I tipped my head back to show him my throat, which I like, and took a long gulp.

'I'll get another,' he said.

So I was left with his lager in one hand, which still tasted bitter, and my too sweet cider in the other, and Jackie, Ella and irrelevant boy looking at me. Ella was smiling, but only with one side of her mouth, irrelevant boy was checking me out and Jackie looked a bit concerned. She took me to one side.

'He's a bit of a shit,' she said. 'Andy.'

'How do you know?'

'I know.'

'I don't care.'

We danced slowly. He had a hand on my shoulder, and a hand holding a cold bottle of Stella in my back. I'd put both my drinks down. I turned my face up towards him, and he lowered his on to mine. His lips squashed on mine, his lower lip pressing between my lips, but I wasn't thinking about the kiss, I was thinking how easy this had turned out to be, how some make-up, a few arbitrary words and some pretend confidence could lead to Andy Butter kissing me in front of everyone. I pressed up against him, wanting to feel whether I'd made him hard, and he put his hand on the back of my head and pushed his tongue into my mouth. After a couple of seconds of that I was having trouble breathing, so I put my hands over his ears and lifted his head off me. 'You're a great kisser,' I said, because I know boys' confidence can be fragile too. He was smiling with both sides of his mouth. He wasn't having any trouble with his confidence, as far as I could tell.

There was something going on at the door. We both looked over. Jackie was talking to my brother, who was pointing at me.

'Who's that?' Andy was still holding me.

'No idea,' I said, trying to hide behind his shoulder.

But Jackie and Sean were coming over.

'Did you invite your brother?' said Jackie.

'Yeah, sorry.' Andy was disengaging. I couldn't keep my arms round his neck without looking stupid, so I let go of him.

Jackie was looking at Sean like he'd already said something funny to her. How had he managed that? 'It's fine,' she said. A glance at me then back to him. 'Rosa's told me all about you.'

'She's told me all about you too.'

They were both lying. I wanted to say *You're both lying*, but I didn't think they'd care. Then Jackie did something surprising. She took my hand, said 'Excuse me' to Sean, and led me to the kitchen.

She backed me up against the dishwasher, which had three candles on it. I could feel their heat through my top. I was trying to remember the last time anyone had held my hand. 'OK,' she said. She started talking quickly, like she had a lot to say but only five seconds to say it. 'Andy's been sleeping with Ella, but she chucked him because he slept with Jess. Just thought you should know. You could do better, like his mate for instance, did you fancy him? I could introduce you, only I reckon slow down a bit with him, because he's the quiet type, you know? He actually notices if you've got a brain, so he should like you.' She took a breath, but didn't pause long enough for me to speak. 'And where do you stand on the whole friends fancying your brother thing? Because I think Sean is gorgeous. Tell me about him.'

'Jackie, I think my top's on fire.'

'Oh, Jesus! Sorry, sorry.'

We moved, she patted my back, apologising. I realised she was a bit drunk.

'Sean told me he'd never be my friend.'

'He didn't? When'd he say that?'

'When he was nine.'

Jackie stared at me a moment. Then she tipped back her head, like me drinking lager, and laughed. It was a happy, spontaneous sound, loud enough to make someone look into the kitchen, wondering what was going on. She leaned on the sink for support, and even when she stopped she was still grinning at me. 'You're funny,' she said. 'I knew you'd be funny.' When we went back into the sitting room, Andy was talking to Jess, who'd just arrived, and Sean was talking to Ella. Irrelevant boy, aka Andy's mate, aka Josh, was trying to pretend he liked standing on his own. So we went to talk to him.

It was another cold night, but this time I had my big over-coat on. The air was sharp-edged in my lungs, but it sobered me up. I walked towards my house, but I wasn't going home yet. I kept walking, past the house and towards the park, but I wasn't going there either. I never did understand what a desire path was meant to be, but maybe I was on one now, had been on one all evening, going off my usual route, striking off to some different place. The street lights dropping orange pools on the pavement, the scatter of stars overhead. I felt like the star in my own drama, walking down the empty street at one in the morning, following a foolish impulse. I had a sense that uncle Frank was my audi-ence, and that he was pleased, because I felt like I filled my skin, and belonged in the world.

Cole's lights were on. He keeps odd hours. I knocked on his door.

He was taken aback to see me, but was too busy being cool to show much surprise. He let me in.

'Sean said you fancy me.'

He'd made me a coffee and sat me down, and now he was giving me a speculative look. I filed it under expres-sions to learn.

'Did Sean tell you I fancy him?'

I shrugged. 'We're a good-looking family.'

Cole laughed. It was the second time in the evening I'd

made someone laugh, and this time it was on purpose. 'Always good to see you,' he said. 'But why are you here? You're not expecting to sleep with me, are you?'

'I'm going to sleep with Josh Reynolds,' I said. 'At least I might. I just wanted to ask you a question.'

He waited. There was some moody music playing and I could smell the lingering floral aroma of a joint. Josh might be thinking about me right now; Jackie might too, for different reasons. Dad was probably asleep; Mum would probably be awake till I came home. Sean would probably be last to leave the party; I was talking to Cole. I was about to ask Cole what brothers were for, and he was about to tell me. I didn't expect him to know, but that was all right, because it wasn't a question which had one correct answer. I paused before I asked the question, because I'd stumbled on to a perfect moment, the whole evening had been leading up to it, and now I wanted to see if I could cheat the ungenerous gods who are in charge of these things and stretch it, because I'm old enough to know that perfect moments almost never happen in the realm of the possible, and they should be cherished.

2000: HIATUS

BILL EATS AS if he's making a point, his jaws forceful and determined. Lamb. I make that meat tender as butter, and he still chews loudly. The children are finishing. I'm steering half a new potato through gravy, I'm watching the potato as if it's a delicate operation, then I look up and say 'I'll be leaving.' Bill stops chewing and looks at me, stares at me with his forehead all furrows.

He always claims he asked me on a date after I squeezed his thigh. It's one of those lines that slips quickly from funny to familiar, and then becomes irritating. I was a physio, he was a Sunday morning footballer with a strained hamstring. He sat on the couch in his shorts while I stood beside him and probed. I told him to slap frozen peas on it morning and evening and lay off sport for two weeks. Then I noticed he was smiling.

I was in a bad mood, it was the aftermath of Dan. I said, 'What?'

He said, 'Do you want to come out Friday?'

It wasn't unusual for me to get asked out by a patient, but I didn't have a policy, I played it by ear. He had a nice smile. He hadn't shaved very well round his Adam's apple.

'Where to?'

'There's a party at work.'

It was his hesitation, the slight nervousness behind the smile. If there's one thing I can't stand it's a brash man. I was aware of my hands still lying on his thigh, soft and useless now, like gloves.

I moved my hands. 'Sure,' I said. 'Yes, sure.'

The thing with lamb stew is it has to be slow. That business about meat surrendering itself from the bone, it's true. Let the fat on the meat, which has all the taste in it, melt. Let the tight fibres on the meat gently loosen, let the juices ease out of the vegetables, and let all the different flavours you've put in the pot percolate together. The smell will fill the kitchen. Put your face in the steam and inhale it.

'Brown food,' says Sean, unimpressed.

I slice a chunk of lamb fillet with the side of my fork. 'Tender,' I say to him. I spear the meat and point the fork at Bill. 'Tender.'

Rosa's pissed off with me, but that's nothing new. God knows what goes on in Sean's head. I take my wine into the kitchen. Bill is standing at the sink drying dishes in that thorough, jerky way, all elbows, as if he's trying to throttle something before it can make a sound.

I attempt to reassure. 'It's only a course.'

'Then why did you say you were leaving us?'

'I am leaving, for five days. And it's about me. Not you or Sean or Rosa.'

'A course?'

'Poetry.'

He puts down a dry plate. It could have used a rinse, but I'll keep that to myself. He looks at it, looks at me. 'I don't understand.'

My muscles relax and untense as I leave. I hadn't realised they needed to relax and untense until I got on the M6 and began to accelerate away, southwards, eighty miles an hour in the middle lane, Cheshire flat and dull on either side, the October sky flat and grey above. Then I realised my shoulders were lowering and I was gently moving my head from side to side. There's something wonderful about a road spooling into the distance, about space and sky all around, about being between places and uncontactable. You feel, even though you're driving, even though you're in charge of the car, that you're giving yourself up to something. Take me away, road, take me somewhere else. Anywhere will do.

John Denver is on Radio 2. 'I'm Leaving On A Jet Plane.' The reception's scratchy and the song's hideous in the first place, but I sing along all the same, loud and inaccurate. Does this count as poetry?

At the service station, I look at the Road Atlas while I eat a dish of ice cream. There's a small stain on the plastic surface of my table, and I pick at it with a fingernail. I'm keeping track of sensations. Cold ice cream in my coffee-warm mouth. The airlessness of the car. The ocean sound of the wind at the open window. This is what poets do, they observe. Bill's face when I said *I'll be leaving*. And Sean's face, and Rosa's. Why did I say it? Because I wanted to hear what the words sounded like, and see how my family would react. I observed them, and I observed, inside myself, a drop of pleasure. It's good to surprise people who assume they know you as well as an old sweater.

So I head back to the car still feeling pretty good, crossing the car park and enjoying being somewhere unfamiliar, but as soon as I'm back on the motorway, I know that something's not right. Eighty miles an hour, middle lane, some new county, less flat but still dull, on either side. But something's not right. I've been fired so far by the exhilaration of leaving, but now my mind has moved on to where I'm going. What will the tutor be like? Bearded and drunken? And the students. Lecherous men, and women in floaty skirts, all of them much more experienced at poetry than me. I haven't written a poem in ten years. I wrote one for Rosa's birthday when she was seven, and found the experience so depressing I gave up poetry the same day. They'll look at me, frizzy-haired, nearly fifty, clearly ill at ease, and they'll wonder what I'm doing there.

The last reading I went to involved poetry and jazz. I walked into the club and recognised the scene immediately as the life I'd once mapped out for myself. One of them, anyway. The one where I'd be dressed all in black, smoking, drinking black coffee, listening to the rhythmic burp of the double bass with my cool friends. We found a table. I was wearing my black V-neck and cropped black chinos. I'd bought ten Marlboro. Bill was loving it. He said 'Why don't we do this more often?' He smirked at my cigarette, stole a drag, and said I looked like an undergraduate. He meant it in a nice way. We settled in for an unusual evening, feeling pleased with ourselves.

Then the poet came on. I enjoyed the bits between the poems but not the poems themselves. She had little explanations, biographical fragments and polished self-deprecating jokes, all of which I liked, but the poems made me feel dense. Bill was sitting there nodding, but I could see he wasn't enjoying it either, so when she announced a short break we slipped away, a bit hasty and furtive, like guests who have blundered into the wrong party.

Maybe I haven't done enough planning. Maybe I should have cut my hair, and bought new clothes. But what clothes? A floaty skirt? A black top with thin straps? Something purple? I'm losing confidence and my courage is ebbing. Once I dreamt about killing a man, and swimming the Channel. Now I'm scared of poets. What's become of me?

It's about an hour to my destination. I'm having second thoughts about going forward, and I can't bear to go back.

§

Turn on to the Promenade, drive down it a little way, find a space. And there's the Channel. Twenty miles of it. I sit and stare for a while, and then I'm out of the car, down the steps and on to the beach. Pebbles chinking like small change as my feet sink into them. If crossing the beach is hard work, what would the swim be like? I stop at the water's edge. I was serious about this once, I was going to do it. It looks easy enough today, like I could strip off here and now and swim across. I stare and stare, looking for the shadowy outline of land across the water.

'One night, I think, but my plans aren't clear yet.'

She smiles, unperturbed, and does something to her screen. She's wearing a green blazer and a white shirt. Sometimes I'm attracted to a life which involves a uniform, and a smile, and a few set tasks. She asks if I need help with my luggage, then singsongs her directions to the lift. My key appears to be a credit card. It's a long time since I've been in a hotel, in this country.

We left the kids with Bill's mother and went to the Lake District. A four-poster bed and a glimpse of Windermere. It rained so we stayed in, and Bill asked if he could tie me up. He tied my left wrist to one of the posts with his black woollen scarf, but I couldn't comfortably reach the other. He took the jam out of the doll's house jar that came at breakfast and spread it on my nipples. I probably laughed more than I should have.

I share the lift with a tall man who catches my eye in the mirrored wall and smiles. He's wearing a weathered leather jacket. I smile back, my mind still tangled in bondage and jam. I think he's about to say something but we're at my floor, so I nod and leave him.

A large double bed, a television, a mini-bar. Better facilities I'm sure than the poetry course is providing. They'll probably be doing introductions now, sitting in a circle, discreetly sizing each other up. I'd planned to be Stella for the week, because it's a name I've always admired.

Hello, I'm Stella. I did an Open University course recently and it rekindled my interest in poetry. I have a tangle inside me that poetry might unravel, and put into some sort of order. Wallace Stevens wrote a poem called Ideas of Order, but I'm not sure what it meant.

At that point I'd have looked at the tutor, and the spotlight would have moved off me.

I'm not sure about *rekindled*.

Room Service brings my sandwiches. It's a spotty boy, in a green blazer and a white shirt. He's about Sean's age, and is feeling chatty.

'Here on business?' he says.

'I'm a poet.'

'Can you do that, for a job?'

I tell him it's precarious, but satisfying. I like that, it sounds attractive, so I repeat it thoughtfully. 'Yes, precarious, but satisfying.' It was a mistake to repeat it, it sounds slightly less good, like a weather forecast. Sunshine, but showers.

'How's your job?' I try.

'Honestly?'

I nod.

'Shit.'

I give him a pound, and he leaves. So much for the uniform, the smile and the few set tasks.

I find myself pacing. This isn't any of the lives I once planned. Cool friends in the smoky club; gold medal for the hundred metres freestyle; pavement cafe with my Italian lover in Rome. Instead I have a warm, dull room, nothing on telly, dry sandwiches with Pringles, a glimpse of the sea from the window. I might have made a wrong decision, if you can even dignify it with the word *decision*. Fourteen steps from the door to the window. Curtains striped in beige and a muted red. It's more of a retreat, a running away.

I pick up the phone and dial.

'Rosa? Hello, darling.'

She asks me how the course is.

'It's going to be fine.' I'd prepared for the question, and answer without a beat.

'Mum, why'd you say you were leaving like that? We thought you were really leaving. And why didn't you tell us about this course? Why'd you spring it on us?'

I thought I'd got away with it. I thought they were all going to pretend it was normal for me to come to a snap decision without taking them into account. Families can do that, overlook odd behaviour, pretend it's not odd, or it's not significant.

'Are you all right, Mum? Because lately, I don't know … Is there anything you want to talk about?'

'I'm fine,' I say. 'It's just what I said to your father, it's just something for me.'

There's a silence. She's waiting for me to clarify, which is a trick she's learnt from me. I don't.

'Is he there?'

'He's at a film.'

'You didn't fancy it?'

'I'm waiting for a phone call.'

So we talk briefly about her putative new boyfriend, Carl from the greengrocer's. We don't exactly talk. She rations me a certain amount of information and opinion, and I try to respond helpfully. I've already been accused of being prejudiced and snobby on this issue.

'Love you,' I say, finally.

'Shall I give your love to Dad?'

An extra layer of inquiry under the bland words. 'Of course,' I say. 'And to Sean.'

Not pacing now, just standing still, my hand on the cradled phone, draped and forgotten, I notice, like a glove. Decision. I find gin and tonic in the mini-bar, and squirt complementary foam under the hot tap. The bath is frequently my recourse when I'm bored or aimless. More of that relaxing and untensing as I slide my legs in under an alp of bubbles. A sense of unfolding, my shoulders loosening. I move my jaw, as if chewing. Better. Take a deep, slow breath. Better.

How often in my life, I wonder, am I walking around unaware that I'm holding myself unrelaxed and tense, as if braced for a blow? What I need now is for my head to follow the example of my muscles, and that tangle to resolve itself into something legible. Everything seems to be effort: deciding to go on the course, telling the family, leaving, deciding not to go on the course. It's as if with each move I make I have to consult the Road Atlas again, and find a new route—*This must be it, this must be what I want*—but the map is faulty, or I'm misreading it.

I sip gin, cold all the way down, and shrug deeper into the water.

Next day I phone the course, tell them not to expect me. And now I'm in the clear. My family think I'm shacked up in a house in the countryside with a bunch of poets, but I'm not, I'm somewhere else. I'm somewhere else for up to a week, and not a soul in my world knows where I am.

What to do? Sit in my room, eat room service and watch TV? Take a bracing walk along the Prom? I counsel people like me. I can hear myself: *Imagine yourself in a situation entirely without connections or responsibilities. A hiatus. What do you do?*

I do this: have lunch in a veggie café. Juice and soup while reading the paper. Browse a bookshop. Browse a hippie shop selling candles and bright fabrics. Browse a clothes shop. Go for the bracing walk. Stare at the water for a long time, throw stones at it, and then have an ice cream.

When I get back to my room there is still a distressingly large part of the day left. I watch a quiz show, read my book, and spend some time staring at the door to my room. I imagine opening it and finding not a hotel corridor, not the banal English coast, not even England perhaps, but somewhere fresh and unexpected. A busy street, where a stranger would notice me looking back and forth, smiling, and would pause.

I head down to the bar, angry with myself.

The man from the lift glances my way, and I give him half a smile. That's all it takes. Next thing, he's at my table, with his beer and another glass of white. He's got stubby fingers and his lips are dry. He's wearing a pale blue shirt under his distressed leather.

'Seems wrong,' he says, 'the two of us sitting on our own.'

Ten years ago I was in that hotel with Bill. Wedding anniversary. Him tying me to the bed, in a half-hearted sort of way. Twenty-five years ago, I was a different person. The one who was going to murder Dan, and swim the Channel. That was then. Twenty-five years ago, when I was impetuous.

He's still standing at my table. He's a confident man, and I think he's probably too fond of his leather jacket, but there's nothing brash about him.

'Join me,' I say.

'Anthony,' he says.

I shake his hand. 'Stella.'

Here's an idea. When I get home I could tell Bill my name's Stella. 'Don't be stupid, Ali,' he'll say. I'll say 'Who's Ali? My name's Stella.' I won't answer to Ali, I'll have no idea what he's talking about. I must just be someone who looks like her. I'll ask him, 'What was she like, this Ali?' When he tells me, I'll shake my head. 'No, doesn't sound like me.' We'll be complete strangers, we'll have to get to know each other, see if we like each other. We'll have to start again.

Anthony works for a publisher of videogames. There's a small but promising creative team based near here, apparently. He has to decide whether his firm should swallow them up. He pretends to be interested in my thoughts on this, so we discuss it for a while, then talk about the town, and how living in the South compares to living in the North, and he turns that into how it feels to be hundreds of miles from home. I point out that he's only about fifty miles from London.

He leans forward and smiles. It's mostly on one side of his mouth and his eyes are resting on mine. 'Pedant,' he says.

The smile tells me everything I need to know. I lean forward too, and until my lips meet his I'm not sure what I'm about to do. The kiss lasts three seconds, and then I move my face away from his and apologise. He leans back too and I mention Bill and we take slow steps away from that moment. Because I am not impetuous any more. Decisions come slowly; clarity arrives, if it arrives at all, unexpectedly.

Down to the beach again, pebbles chinking like small change again. I strip to the swimming costume I've just bought. My teeth begin to chatter. The cold of the English

Channel grips my calves, laps at me and slides up me, making me gasp and then shout as I plunge in, ungainly, before I lower my face into the water and carve forwards with a splashy front crawl. I remember standing on a high diving board, twenty-five years ago, a question arriving in my head. *What am I going to do?*

There isn't much to swimming the Channel, besides stamina and desire. One hand after the other, breaths every other stroke, try to ignore the cold, swim around jellyfish and floating garbage, wait for big ships to move ponderously out of the way; there isn't much to it at all. But I've only gone a little way before I turn back, splashing swiftly towards the shore. I dry quickly, pull clothes on over my damp costume, sneeze. My name isn't Stella, my name is Ali, and I know that swimming the Channel doesn't belong in my future. Nor does Anthony, nor does poetry, and nor does lamb stew, no matter how slow, no matter how tender.

2000: GLADNESS

WHAT WOULD HE *do if she left him?* He should have a plan, because sometimes it felt more than possible. Never imminent, but sometimes looming. Bill shook himself, wriggling his head and his shoulders, trying to prevent his back from seizing up. Flexed his hands on the steering wheel. He tried to assess himself, see if there was anything he could do to hold up his end of the relationship a little better. Be more sensitive to her moods; try not to correct her, unless it was really necessary; not bite his lips. Right now, for instance, he was chewing the inside of his cheek. He stopped. Then started again.

What would he do? He'd try advertising. Or, more likely, replying to adverts. He'd look in the *Guardian* or the *Independent*, he'd find someone a bit younger than himself, someone with GSOH who didn't sound over-confident, and who didn't seem to be employing coy euphemisms for their obesity. 'Hi,' he said, talking to his glanced-at reflection, 'Bill Dax. This is embarrassing, isn't it?' Oh, God. The effortful attempt to be casual and amusing, the wry acknowledgement of their situation which might so easily sound pitiable. *I don't want to be lonely.* That would be the subtext. The agonising, obvious subtext. *Help me not to be lonely, and I'll help you.*

Enough. That kind of day-dreaming he could do without. If she left him, he'd be fine. He'd probably meet someone through work. And anyway, she wasn't going to leave him. The traffic was slowing. With another glance in the mirror, he took his foot off the gas. The wrinkles round his eyes seemed to be getting deeper, he noticed. More like crevices than wrinkles. He lifted his left eyelid, and studied his reflection, examining the twiggy veins approaching his iris.

When he looked down again, he was approaching a stationary car at sixty-five miles an hour.

He stamped on the brake. Approaching. Wrong word. He was *hurtling* towards it. A Rover, hazard lights blinking. The brake squashed against the floor. Sixty-five had never seemed so fast. Traffic blocking all three lanes ahead. Cars to his left. He couldn't swerve on to the hard shoulder. His breath came in gasps. His neck muscles so tight it was hard to turn his head. The road between them was vanishing. He'd seen the traffic slowing, the flow becoming sludgy, he'd taken his foot off the gas, but he hadn't realised everything had stopped. Was vanity going to kill him? The depth of his wrinkles. He made a sound, some sort of strangled throat noise.

It was a Rover, its hazard lights were blinking, and the road between them was vanishing.

The traffic still wasn't moving. Bill checked his watch. He should have been at the studio twenty minutes ago. He remembered a Rosa-ism: *Way to impress the new producer, Dad.* He turned off the ignition.

No one apparently had noticed his personal drama. He'd stopped inches away from a collision and slumped back in his seat, expecting the Rover driver to storm out and rant at him. Nothing. He'd looked at the cars pulling up sedately on either side of him. No one was staring. He'd cheated death, and no one had noticed. It wasn't even anecdote material—he'd go to his meeting and not even mention it.

The letter, addressed to All Writers, had said that Claire

was *very disappointed* with the last story conference, that no one had sent in stories beforehand, that *discussion had not been constructive* and the story office were left with *gaping holes* to fill. He must have looked surprised as he read it, because Sean was staring at him and Rosa asked him what was wrong.

'No, nothing. Slap on the wrist from Claire. Not just for me. All writers.'

Sean smirked. 'Not working hard enough?'

'You'd know all about that.' He turned to Rosa. 'Why aren't you at school yet?'

'Study period. What if I wanted to get into TV, Dad? Could you help?'

'Do you want to?'

She shrugged, pushed her lips out. 'No.'

'If you want to get into television, get good A levels, and get a degree.'

The words *Not like your brother* wallowed in his mouth, unspoken.

'I want to be an artist.' She took a bite of toast. 'Are you going to get sacked?'

Funny how it interested her, but didn't seem to worry her in the least. He resisted the urge to shrug back at her. 'Claire's just making her presence felt.'

Sean paused as he was leaving the room. 'Know what you should do? Tell her where she can stick her letter.'

Bill slammed the car door, stretched, and shielded his eyes. The patchwork of cars stretched ahead until the motorway wound out of his view. A moment of unease, almost vertigo, standing in the middle lane, turning his back on the queue behind him. What if he wandered a few steps away, and the blockage suddenly cleared, leaving him to dodge speeding, blaring traffic? He put his hand on the bonnet,

warm in the sun and textured with grime, balancing himself. He could see at least half a mile ahead. No movement.

Nothing sudden was going to happen, nothing unexpected. But as soon as this thought arrived, he questioned
it. He'd just nearly died—that had been sudden. And his
children had grown up, suddenly. He felt unsure of Ali, suddenly. Time played tricks—it felt like only yesterday they'd
been passionate, and entirely confident. Only yesterday
she'd told him she was pregnant with Sean, and given him
a scarf he still had somewhere. And yesterday he'd felt fairly
secure on *Calder's Road*, now he wasn't sure where he stood.

'Do you know where we are?'

She'd just got out of a small green Fiat. He looked
puzzled.

'I mean junctions.'

'Near Leeds. Between twenty-six and twenty-seven.'

'I am going to be so late.'

She shoved a hand through her hair. He saw bitten
fingernails.

'Me too,' he said, 'but when something like this happens,
there's no point fighting it, you have to just go with it.'

'That's very nice, but I've got a meeting.'

She took out her mobile and punched numbers. Something about her relaxed him. She was about ten years
younger than him, more smartly dressed (green jacket,
black skirt), much more anxious. He'd nearly died, and he
was calmer than her. He could see her in a magazine. Not a
model, but a woman illustrating a feature, sitting in a cafe
with an expresso and a group of attractive friends.

Yesterday, he'd met Ali for the first time. She stood over
him and massaged his hamstring. She wore her blue-edged
physio's uniform. Her thumbs, digging in, made him gasp
and laugh. She wanted to know what he was laughing at.

She'd paused, leaving her hands on his thigh, and he felt an embarrassing erection pushing at his shorts. 'Do you want to come out with me?' he blurted. He claimed there was a party at work at the end of the week. She moved her hands and straightened, and he thought she was going to say No, or possibly just pretend he hadn't spoken. She said 'Sure.' Casual, as if she'd been expecting the invitation. 'Yes, sure.' He felt almost annoyed at the routine way she'd agreed. He wanted some kudos for the audacity he'd shown in asking her, the aplomb with which he'd carried it off. There was no party. He had to phone round his friends, press-gang them into turning up in his one bedroom flat. 'This is what self-employed people mean,' he told Ali, 'when they say a party at work.' She laughed. It was the first time he'd made her laugh.

'My name's Gina.' She was putting away her mobile.

'Bill.'

'Sorry if I was snappy.'

He shook his head. 'Last thing you want is some jerk telling you to relax.'

He told her he was a scriptwriter on *Calder's Road*. She said she didn't watch it. He assured her it had mostly a younger demographic, although quite a few grannies watched, and it also attracted a gay following.

'Sorry,' he said. 'I sound like the PR department. What do you do?'

'I work for Abbey National.'

He couldn't think of a response to this. They both looked at their watches, then at the clogged traffic. Far away there was some tentative movement, although it wasn't clear if it was leading to anything.

She studied him. 'Are you gay?'

'Me? No.'

'Married?'

'Nope.'

That's what he said, *Nope*, like a cowboy. He didn't hesi-
tate, and he looked her straight in the eye as he spoke. She
had glossy dark hair framing a round face, thin oval frames
in her glasses, a biggish nose. Deep-red lips. Ali never wore
make-up.

She was smiling at him, a little embarrassed now. 'You
can ask me a question if you like.'

'You married?'

'No. And I don't make a habit of chatting men up.'

She was chatting him up? He nodded at her car, parked
by the central reservation. 'I can see you like to travel in the
fast lane.' What? What did he mean by that?

There was definitely movement now, rippling towards
them, the tight braid of traffic slowly fraying. She handed
him her card. 'Call me.' And she was gone. He wondered if
she'd bought the green jacket to match her car.

'All we've had on screen these last few weeks,' said Claire,
'is Calder's regrets and Ellie's guilt, and frankly it's getting
boring. I want something fresh.'

She held one end of her biro and tapped the other on the
table like a small hammer. The sofas were set at right-
angles in the corner and they were too low. She was on one,
leaning over the coffee table, looking like she was prepar-
ing for a sprint. He was on the other, eyes on her biro,
muscles throbbing around the base of his spine.

'Regret and guilt,' she said. 'Sounds like a Bergman film.
Regret's a stooped, hooded figure, dressed in, what, beige,
and carrying . . . what would Regret be carrying?'

She was looking at him, waiting. Raised eyebrows, a sardonic twist to the lips. Great. Now his career depended on coming up with witty banter. His mind was blank.

'A harp,' he said. 'Regret would be carrying a harp.'

A pause, and Claire's smile diminished by fifty per cent. 'OK.'

Bill knew he'd let her down. No place at the table of flashing wits for him. He should have worked up his near-crash into an anecdote after all, elaborated a bit, exaggerated. He was about to shift his position, lean forward a little into her space, when a wasp landed on the back of his hand.

'Anyway,' she said, 'I'm glad you could come in and see me.'

She became business-like. The wasp was crawling towards his knuckles. He tried to ignore it as Claire rattled off her points, tapping the biro for emphasis. Obviously the story office needed a new broom. And the cast needed a clear-out. And some of the writing team—this was hardly a controversial point—was dead wood. Not Bill though. She wanted Bill's input. She respected what Bill had done on the show, and she respected his experience. *Dr Who.* Christ, *Juliet Bravo.* What the show needed was a disaster, could Bill pitch something?

Bill began to open his mouth —a car crash had sprung to mind—but she hadn't paused. 'How do you feel,' she said, 'about trains? A train crash, a train comes off the rails and ploughs up a platform on which is standing the best part of our cast. In fact, the worst part of our cast. Maybe they're seeing someone off? Or better, could it be a wedding? Can you have a wedding on a station platform? I don't see why not. What I'm suggesting is bride, full wedding dress, bridegroom, top hat and tails, guests, Intercity 125. Can you see it?'

The wasp paused at his knuckle, turned round, stung him and took off, heading for a fortuitously open window and the broad blue sky beyond.

Little fucker. He was back on the motorway, heading home. Little fucker. His hand was swelling like a fat red glove. Sausage fingers, puffy skin. Didn't disturb it, didn't frighten it. Little fucker just landed, stung him and flew. He shook his hand, tried licking it. He felt suddenly beset, as if his life was turning into trite sit-com. Work problems, marriage problems, feisty teenage daughter, layabout son, and a strange woman's business-card in his pocket. He didn't want to turn into a bewildered television Dad, worried by age and unspecific anxiety, on a bumbling search for something, clarification, some sort of missing gist to his life.

The last thing he'd really enjoyed doing was talking on the radio about the show. 'Think of three things to say, and say them', his PR minder told him. 'Never mind what he asks you. And make at least two of them funny.' He sat at a round table, leaning into a microphone, and focused on the presenter, a calm man with a monkish haircut called Paul. Paul said 'Forget about the audience, just have a conversation with me.' But Bill knew there were about a million people listening to him, once you added in the evening repeat. A million people. He'd loved that. He found fluency and became his best self, pinpointing what worked about the show and satirising what didn't, making Paul laugh, making, perhaps, a million people laugh. It wasn't some character's voice, someone else's storyline, some fictional environment, it was just him, Bill Dax, sitting in a stuffy little studio and entertaining the nation. That was the last thing he'd really enjoyed. It was over a year ago.

꙳

She held his wounded hand in one of hers and stroked camomile lotion into his tender flesh. She used two finger-tips, moving them up and down between the tendons, gliding them over the lotion so that they barely touched the skin. Hairs flattened and parted beneath her fingerprints, her bitten nails.

'Better?' she said.

He nodded. 'Better. You're good at this.'

She smiled. He liked the easy way she accepted compli-ments.

'You did go to school today, did you?'

'Da-ad.' She extended it, like she often did, into two syl-lables, the short word not substantial enough to express her feelings. He liked that too, liked the way she moved her head to the rhythm of the word, and how, saying it, she pulled back her mouth, almost smiling. Her face still smooth, undamaged by time.

'How was the meeting?'

'Claire respects my work. Wants me to come up with a big accident to kill half the cast.'

'Great.'

He'd felt disappointed. He walked out of her office, clenching and unclenching his hand, imagining how he'd feel if he'd just been sacked. *Bill, your scripts have become a bit lacklustre, I think maybe your heart's not in it.* He'd have felt lib-erated. He'd never intended to write soap opera, he'd intended to write films. Serious films, appreciated by crit-ics, which found unexpected commercial success and led to enquiries from major Hollywood studios. Perhaps if she'd sacked him he'd have returned to that old, almost exhausted ambition. In his twenties he'd craved success and

recognition, in his thirties he'd made a painful accommo-
dation with, in his own terms, failure. Now he was
forty-nine, and there was nothing to stop him trying again,
only this time without the pain. He no longer craved anything, really. He didn't ask for much at all. A little esteem
from his family and friends. A small, but unambiguous por-
tion of gladness in his heart.

Gina Wilson. It was simple black on white, Helvetica ten
point, good quality paper. It smelt of something other than
itself. A hint of leather from her wallet perhaps, or maybe
it had been jostled by some musky perfume in her bag? He
had a brief vision of Gina laying a few cards on a table and
spraying them with an atomiser, on the off-chance that
she'd run into a suitable man. That was him. A suitable
man. Gina sized him up swiftly and found him suitable.
What would he do if Ali left him? How about, what would
she do, if he left her?

He had the card at his nose, smelling it again, trying to
inhale every particle of scent, when Ali walked in, wearing
two towels.

'Are you changing?'

He looked at himself in the mirror, saw an innocent face.
'Should I?'

She didn't answer. She was taking the turbanned towel
off her head, giving her hair a last squeeze with it.

'What's that?'

'Nothing. The producer's card.' He wished he hadn't said
that. Ali knew the producer's name was Claire.

'I nearly died,' he said.

'What?'

'On the motorway. Not that nearly, but it was scary.'

The bare few words didn't do justice to the experience.
The last time he'd nearly died was on a Greek island. Two

thugs, one with a knife, attacked him, and a man called Loomis intervened. Their first anniversary, twenty-three years ago.

Ali was unwinding the towel from her torso, assuming there was no more to say about the motorway and the not very close encounter with death. She turned on the radio, only just loud enough to hear.

'Why were you smelling the card?'

'I love the smell of paper.' His face in the mirror was looking less innocent, more trapped. 'It smells of . . .' He couldn't think what it smelt of.

'Paper?'

She stood naked, looking at him, puzzled. Yesterday, he was a teenage boy, trying to conjure an image of a naked woman in his mind.

'Remember our first anniversary?' he said.

'Are you all right?'

Time, at once sluggish and nimble, had landed him here, in middle-age, entering sit-com land, his ambitions expired. But he was alive, at least. He put the card into his chest pocket, searched for something to say, something that had nothing to do with the lies and cliches of television, and said it:

'I love you?'

But it came out as a question. She smiled anyway, and kissed him briefly, leaning over him, her hand over his pocket, over his heart, and the music on the radio whined on quietly, like the soundtrack to the kind of film he would never choose to see.

2001: HOUDINI

L IZ HAD ARMPIT stubble, moles, a BCG scar, and her labia
were thick and uneven, like misshapen ears. She smelt
of her body as well as her perfume, and Sean kissed most of
her. Held her. Loved her. Loved her. Loved her. All the time
the sound of the traffic rising and falling through the open
window as the lights changed on the road outside her flat,
loud and quiet, loud and quiet, and the sound reminded
them that the world had not been shut out, that they had
not escaped it, but were a fortunate morsel of it.

He stretched and groaned, pulling the sheet back over
them, rearranging their contours, cold now.

Once he was comfortable he said, 'London.'

She nodded.

'I can't wait.'

'Me neither,' she yawned.

'Escape.'

She raised herself on an elbow. He saw three moles on
her bicep. Her shoulders slanting towards him. They were
her favourite feature, but not even in his top five. 'You
always call it escape,' she said. 'We're not escaping, we're
moving.'

A pause, long enough to sound like he agreed with her.
Then he sighed. 'Feels like escape to me. Houdini's my
hero, have I told you that?'

She laughed and lay down again. 'I don't think Houdini
would have been scared to tell his parents he was leaving
town.'

Sean started to deny it, then didn't bother.

Me and Liz, me and Liz, me and Liz.

Ali read it, used two fingers to turn the scrap of paper all the way around, then read it again. She was smiling. Sean probably thought he was the first person in the world to be in love. She could see him at his desk, planning to write a card or a note, and these words spilling out instead. *Me and Liz, me and Liz.* Holding his breath, his face close to the paper, his mind full of her. She stared another moment at the jostling, hurried letters, wondering if he was seeing her now, then she dropped the clean T-shirts on his bed and left his room.

Bill's office smelt. It was a cocktail of ink cartridges, the stale water at the bottom of his spider plant, a shirt worn once too often. He had fifteen names on index cards on his desk and he was shifting them around like a General marshalling a very small army. Ali stood in the doorway and watched. Short grey hair, shoulders curved inwards as if to hide what he was doing. He was engrossed. She could lay her hands on his shoulders gently, and he might lean back into her. She could kiss the top of his head, smell his hair, and he might turn and kiss her. The scrape of his chin on her cheek. These are things she might have done once.

She said, 'Do you think anyone else on the team works like this?'

He looked round, surprised to see her. 'No,' he said. 'I'm unique.' He moved one of the index cards next to another. 'Siobhan and Matt, what do you think?'

'What do you mean?'

'For an affair. We want passion, jeopardy, pain. They could give us that.'

He wasn't really asking her, he was asking himself, testing the idea by saying it out loud. She could tell because his eyes weren't focused on her, and his forehead was creased as he considered it.

'Why must it always be about affairs?' she said.

'Because that's what gives us the cover of *TV Quick*.' His voice went deep and dramatic. 'Tonight on *Calder's Road*, Siobhan and Lee remain happily married.' He shook his head. 'Just doesn't work. Plus, it's life, isn't it? Life's rich pattern.'

She looked at the constellation of cards on the desk, imagining all the possible relationships they represented.

'Let's not go tonight,' she said.

'How come? Are you all right?'

Are you all right? It was a question he'd asked more than once lately, and finding a truthful way to answer it seemed unfairly difficult. She took a breath. Ink, stale water, body odour. He was staring at her. She looked up at the skylight above his desk, which was filled with bland, grey sky. 'Just don't fancy it,' she said.

A note of irritation entered his voice. 'Come on, how often do we go out?'

She looked at him again, they stared at each for a moment, then she left him to his plotting.

Houdini's my hero. What did he say that for? Sean was in the library, at a table with an elderly man reading a newspaper. Behind him a young woman was muttering to herself as she ran her finger over the CD rack. Sean had three books beside him and one open in front of him. He was reading up on Houdini, and imagining himself telling Liz. He did this, imagined himself telling her things; it was a sign that he was in love. Other signs: he thought about her all the time; he imagined her with him; he measured his actions against her putative response.

The elderly man noisily turned a page of the newspaper, the young woman made a selection and moved off, Sean kept reading. He'd be an authority on Houdini, he'd be fascinating, pacing up and down while Liz lay on the bed, rapt. He'd gesticulate. *Turns out Houdini worked through metaphor, he'd say. He was popular everywhere, but most of all in countries with repressive regimes. He'd contact every newspaper on his arrival, and arrange a spectacular event. It would always be the same thing—he'd escape from the country's worst prison. He'd be manacled and dumped in a cell, then he'd come bounding out a few minutes later with a big grin, trailing his chains like so much waste paper. People screamed, people actually fainted. And they'd imagine escaping from their own lives.*

Sean imagined his dad seeing him now. He'd laugh. Sean had barely opened a book at school, and now here he was in a library, with the unemployed and the elderly. He wouldn't laugh, he'd snort, that dry little sound which was probably, in fact, the opposite of laughter. But it turns out books aren't so bad, if you get the right relationship with them. You don't get told you *must* read this. You pick something up, put it down, flick through. You start to notice the physical experience of reading—the texture and smell of pages. You find something that doesn't exactly grab your attention but entangles it, and then you sit down and read.

Except now he wasn't reading. His fingers lay on the page, feeling the grainy surface of the paper, his head was bent over the crawling words, but his mind was elsewhere. His mind was on his parents. On telling them he was moving to London, and on what they might have to tell him in return.

꽃

Ali was wondering what to wear tonight. Black top and the linen trousers? Did she feel like putting on a dress? While she was wondering, she was emptying every cupboard in the kitchen. Sean was out, Rosa was at college, Bill was working; she might as well do something useful.

Tins, sugar and flour, pasta and rice, plates, glasses, mugs, cutlery. She took off her sweater and had a glass of water. Cereal, tea towels, foil, cling film, sellotape, scissors, old wrapping paper, bin bags, bowls. She rested a moment, caught sight of her reflection in the glass of the oven door. Middle-aged woman in old pink T-shirt. Could use a haircut. And why was she out of breath? She could put on the black top and the linen trousers, but she'd still be middle-aged, unfit and have unruly hair. A spanner, the Magimix, a ball of string, a pile of guarantees and instructions for various appliances, a balloon, a wayward book of stamps and a photograph.

A photograph. Ali stopped what she was doing. Her and Bill, over twenty years ago, a fresh-faced couple she felt she barely knew, on a Greek island. The sun sinking into the sea behind them. The young woman in the photograph won swimming tournaments. She wouldn't get out of breath doing some tidying. She didn't need a haircut either. She had Rosa's hair and Sean's nose. She was laughing, and holding the young man's hand.

Everything was out now, on the work-top and the table. It looked like Ali was erecting cities around the kitchen, compact cities with curved walls and uneven skylines. Disturbed clouds of dust floated down over everything.

She surveyed her work with satisfaction. Every cupboard was empty. The bare interiors, larger than expected, hinted

at the possibility of a more organised, perhaps more aus-
tere life. Things could be different. She surveyed her work,
then went into the sitting room, picked up a magazine, sat
down and began to read. Stretched on the sofa by the
window, a view of the valley to her right, a banal article
resting on her lap. She skim-read for ten minutes, then
paused between paragraphs, and wondered what Rosa was
doing. She'd been talking lately about a teacher at her Sixth
Form College. Gregory. And Sean. Was he with Liz? Ali had
walked into the kitchen a week ago, and found Liz standing there with her fingertips on Sean's cheek. All three had
been awkward, as if she'd found them in a much more
embarrassing position.

The front door opened. Movement. Ali remembered the
state of the kitchen, got up quickly and found Sean there,
looking at empty cupboards and their piled contents.

'Nice one, Mum. Is this a nervous breakdown or just
spring cleaning?'

'It's a fine line,' she said.

Sean had some books under his arm. He was still looking at her work with an impressed smile. 'Thorough.'

She picked up a packet of Basmati. 'Help me put it all
back.'

'You're not going to clean the cupboards first?'

'Can't be bothered.'

They started well, slowed down, paused to put the ket-
tle on, lost interest. Ali made the tea, wondering when
they'd last done this. Just her and Sean. A chance to talk.
She put a hand in her hair, pulling curls out straight then
letting them go, caught herself doing it and stopped, surprised. Was she nervous?

They sat at the table with a small city between them,
composed of blue-edged plates, Christmas wrapping paper

and a box of cling film. Sean had his books in front of him, Ali had the photograph.

'Do you think I look like you,' she said, 'or Rosa?'

Sean took the picture from her and studied it. 'Both,' he said. And then, 'Young love.'

'Speaking of which,' she said, casual, sipping tea, looking at the title of one of his books, 'you and Liz are pretty serious, aren't you?'

He put the photograph down. 'Are you changing the subject?'

'From what?'

Both of them seemed to be having trouble with eye-contact. 'You and Dad.'

'Is that what we were talking about?'

A silence.

'You and Dad,' Sean continued eventually. 'What's going on there?'

This wasn't what she'd intended. She felt outmanoeuvred. 'If there's anything you need to know,' she said, 'I'll let you know.'

Their eyes met and they looked closely but shyly at each other for a few moments, like inquisitive strangers. 'OK.' Sean was on his feet suddenly. 'OK.' And he was gone. Ali finished her tea, gazing at cling film, old wrapping paper, and all the things she still had to clear away.

Obviously, he wasn't scared to tell them he was leaving. It was just the whole situation at the moment. The whole situation at the moment was delicate, and him leaving might be the last thing his parents wanted to think about. Sean was shaving. It could precipitate something, some decisive shift in their relationship. He lowered the razor. And Rosa would probably feel abandoned. Still. A glossy bead of blood appeared on his jawline. Still, it was time. A film tonight, and then that club. After the club he'd tell Liz about Houdini—metaphor, spectacular events, people fainting—and he'd add, like it was nothing, 'Oh, and I told them we're moving to London.' He splashed water on his face, feeling so pleased, it was as if he'd already told them. He tore off a corner of toilet roll and stuck it on his chin. As he did so, his father's face appeared in the mirror. They looked at each other, faces side by side and six feet apart.

'Sorry,' said Bill. 'Didn't know you were in here.'

'I'm done.'

They were speaking through the medium of the mirror, neither moving yet. A moment's pause, and in that moment a memory moved in the air between them. Bill showing Sean how to shave. Centuries ago.

Then Sean turned. 'Dad, there's something I wanted to tell you.'

Bill nodded, his forehead creased as if he was concentrating. 'You're moving out?'

'Yes.'

'About time.'

'You guessed.'

Bill came in and sat on the edge of the bath. 'And moving in with Liz, presumably?' Sean wondered if his parents had been discussing this. *You get him when he comes in, I'll catch him when he's shaving.*

'We're actually moving to London,' he said.

He was watching his father's face, and he saw a movement, a slight shrinking around the jaw, as if he'd experienced a twinge of pain.

'London?'

'Liz knows someone who works in a bookshop. Thinks she can get me a job.'

Blood on his face and a towel round his neck, Sean felt like a boxer. It was just after a fight and part of him, an important part of him, was still out there in the ring, deceiving and pummelling some slow-witted opponent.

'I'm glad,' said Bill, nodding as if to underline his gladness. 'You know what I feel? I feel we've reached a point.' He stopped. That was it, it sounded like half a sentence. *We've reached a point.* Sean nodded. What could he do? He could ask the question he'd asked before. *You and Mum, what's going on there?* He didn't though, he just nodded back at his father. *Have you reached a point?* He didn't ask this either, he said nothing, and Bill got up, said 'Tell me when you've finished,' and walked out. It was a time in that household, in Sean's opinion, when someone was always walking out of a room, leaving a conversation or even a sentence dangling, leaving an absence more eloquent than their presence.

He washed his face and dried it, thinking about Liz again, and telling her. It made it all more concrete. It was really going to happen, they were going to move to London. When he looked at his cut in the mirror, the glass steamed up. He wiped it, grinning at himself. *She makes me short of breath.*

Black top, linen trousers. She came out of her bedroom, hesitated, then went into Sean's. Why? Because he was out. Because he was going to London with Liz. Because she was looking for clues.

She found the book by his bed. *The Escape Artist. A Life of Harry Houdini.* She glanced at it, read a paragraph, sat down and read a page. Something about it caught her attention. She remembered the holiday captured in the photograph.

An American with a strange name. Loomis. He swallowed razors and escaped from chains and clearly fancied her. Her and Bill's first anniversary. Two almost entirely different people. It wasn't that she currently felt chained up, in a straitjacket, upside down in a milk churn, or anything like that. Just that she felt she could be leading a different life. Things could be different.

Sean thought he was the first person in the world to be in love. Which was natural, and healthy. But irritating. She lay down on his duvet, under the picture of a glossy lipped woman almost sucking a microphone. A biscuity smell, faint rumour of his body. She should tell him how she stalked a man once. Sort of stalked him. Followed him down the street with just a towel round her. Then fantasised, at length, about stabbing him to death with a kitchen knife and holding him, tenderly, while the life leaked out of him. *Now that's passion. Don't tell me that's not passion.* Dan was his name. She hadn't thought about Dan for a long time. She sat up. Middle-aged woman with bad hair lies on son's bed thinking about sex. That can't be right. She stood, smoothed her shape out of the duvet. Bill was calling. It was time to go.

'So this guy, all right listen to this, this guy Tom, he leaves his job. Been working there twenty-five years and he's had enough. Just ups and walks out.'

Ali smiled politely, half listening, moving her eyes around the table. Conrad: overweight, a little too hearty, enjoying being centre of attention. Anna: a good friend, hates her job, clearly doesn't much like listening to Conrad's jokes. Michael: funny, argumentative after a few drinks. Grace: too right wing. Paul and Nicola, never met them before. He doesn't say much, she has an irritating laugh. And Bill and Ali. He's drinking a lot tonight, she's not saying much either.

Conrad continued. 'He goes to Alaska. He doesn't want to see anyone ever again. Post is delivered once a fortnight, supplies once a month. It's the middle of nowhere.'

'Is this a joke?' Michael asked. 'Is it a joke, or did it really happen?'

'Sounds like my life,' Bill said. Nicola did her irritating laugh.

Conrad continued. 'After six months there's a knock at the door. Tom opens the door, and this huge guy with a beard is standing there. Hello, he says. I'm Sven, your neighbour. I live forty miles away.'

'Sven?' said Michael. 'Isn't Sven more Norwegian?'

'This fish is gorgeous,' said Grace.

Ali was aware of Paul's eyes on her. He was only half-listening too. She looked at him. Smiled. The thing she noticed about him was his long fingers, cupping his chin. When she smiled he hesitated a moment, as if wondering how to respond, then lowered his hand and smiled back.

'So Sven says, I'm having a party next Saturday, do you want to come? And by this time Tom is feeling a tiny bit lonely, so he says, Sure I'll come. Sven says there'll be some heavy drinking. Tom says, That's fine, I was in business for twenty-five years, I can handle that.'

Nicola, for no obvious reason, laughed her irritating laugh again.

Conrad continued. 'There'll probably be some fighting, said Sven. Tom just shrugs, says That's all right. OK, says Sven, see you there. Oh, by the way, there'll be some wild sex too. Now Tom's definitely interested. He says Great, so what should I wear for this party? Sven says Wear what you like, it'll only be the two of us.'

Bill, Michael and Nicola laughed. Anna rolled her eyes, Grace took an interest in her meal, Ali and Paul smiled politely. Conrad took a big swallow of wine. 'Usually I hate jokes,' he said. Conversation continued, more fragmented. Michael had a theory about a TV presenter involved in a scandal, and when Ali finally turned away, she saw that Paul and Bill were talking about Bach.

'Can't stand him,' said Bill. 'Dry, cerebral. I just haven't got a Maths brain.'

Paul was suddenly passionate. 'No,' he said, 'not at all. It's not about Maths, it's about emotion, it's just a different language for it.'

'OK,' said Bill, good-humoured. 'Trouble is, musically I'm stuck around the time of The Clash and The Stranglers and The Jam.'

'I'm not,' said Ali. 'I have this interest in Bach.'

Bill was looking surprised. 'Do you?'

'I don't know anything about him, but it's like this big area I haven't explored and I think perhaps I want to.'

'It's never too late,' said Paul.

'Exactly,' said Ali. 'It's sort of always there. So when I'm ready, it'll be there.'

Conversation moved on. They talked about the TV presenter, children leaving home, and a film that was on at the Picture House. Somewhere between eleven and midnight Ali said she was tired. Bill looked disappointed but didn't object, and she drove them home.

Ali was on the sofa reading *The Escape Artist*, when the post came. Ehrich Weiss was a Hungarian Jewish immigrant who settled in America, found himself a new name, and reinvented himself. After that everything was different. (Metaphor, spectacular events, people fainting.) She picked up the letters, bills and junk mail and sorted through them, still holding the book, saving her place with a finger. One envelope was handwritten and addressed to her. She took it back to the sofa. Her first client wasn't due for an hour, and Bill was working upstairs. She put down the book and felt the envelope, smelt it, bent it back and forth. She slid her fingernail under the flap and opened it carefully, as if the contents might be delicate. Inside, there was a ticket to a concert in Manchester. Bach's *The Art of Fugue*. There was a note with it—just four words: *Are you ready yet?* She sat on the sofa with her finger in the biography, and stared and stared at the neatly written words, as if they were difficult to decipher.

2001: WAR AND FISH

ROSA BEGAN TO paint fish. It was the colours she liked first, she fell in love with green and silver. Then it was the detail. Tiny, glistening scales, a single watchful eye. It was their mysterious, below-the-surface quality, the way they mooch through their element, slow and curious, then vanish with a flip of the tail. Cole was only planning to spend one morning teaching her techniques with water. In future weeks he was going to pass on to sky, and then landscape and buildings, and finally people. But Rosa got stuck on fish.

Her bedroom filled with pictures. She gave them to her parents and to Gregory. When they were in his bed and he was lying on top of her, she could look to one side and see a crab lurking beneath a rock, look to the other and see minnows swarming in a ray of sunlight.

She dreamt about a tribe in Africa during the Second World War waiting to welcome Hitler. Lines of communication had been opened—the elders of the tribe, naked but for their bright head-dresses, in solemn conference with hot, buttoned-up junior envoys—and an alliance had been established. Now the tribe was waiting to receive Hitler. She arrived, a young German soldier, almost as surprised as they to find herself in such a place. Bemused, they question her. 'Are you,' tentative fingers touch her ill-fitting uniform, 'the Fuhrer?' She says that she is not. There is not much disappointment at this, a touch of tactfully disguised relief in fact, an unlikely Fuhrer she would have made. 'But no doubt you are learned in the craft of war?' She shakes her head unhappily, conscious of her inadequacy. 'Perhaps you can teach us about the psychology of warfare, subtle ways to overcome an enemy?' She has to admit that she cannot. The tribe, unused to contact with outsiders and unsure of etiquette, are embarrassed on her behalf. They think again. 'Are you skilful in the use of weapons, have you brought us the benefits of the superior technology of the Third Reich?' She is not, she has not, she shakes her head sadly. But there is one last question they have for her.

'Can you bake a croissant?'

'Yes. Yes I can, I can bake croissants.'

And so the dream finally ends with, at least, a small sense of accomplishment.

'I dreamt,' she said.

Gregory said something that sounded like 'Ungha', and rolled over slowly, pulling the sheet away from her in a slow movement.

She lay for a while and stared at the ceiling, sheet-less, and then quietly got out of bed. 'Ngh', he said.

Who invented days? she wondered. She had a feeling it was someone called Gregory as it happened, a Pope or an Emperor. The Gregorian calendar. Or maybe that was something else entirely. It was clearly unfair to blame the invention of days on Gregory. The Norse gods, now that she thought of it, may have been responsible. Thor. Thursday.

They drove to her sixth form college, but he dropped her off half a mile from the building. He drove on, parked in the teachers' car park, went to the teachers' common room. She walked the rest of the way, and went to double English. She was eighteen, and not in one of his classes, so their relationship was allowed. Frowned upon perhaps, but allowed. They met at the end of the day for a drink.

'It's an anxiety dream,' he told her. She had remembered all the details, down to the interesting effect of the gaudy plumage on the thin, dusty black bodies of the elders. 'You're worrying about your exhibition.'

She shook her head. 'I'm not.'

He picked a bit of lint off his black polo shirt. 'I expect you had a relative who was a soldier.' Then he looked up at her, discovering that he was curious about her background. As far as he knew she had appeared, a whole creature, from the void.

'No,' she said, 'no soldiers, not recently.'

'What does your father do then?'

'Writes soap opera.'

'And your mother?'

'Psychotherapist.'

'Where did you get this interest in painting?'

He was flinging out the questions without much hesitation now. He had short dark hair and oval glasses, wore a lot of black and tended to hold a student's gaze, challenging them to look away. Rosa paused over his last question, as if examining the words, the temptation to talk about herself, for a hidden hook.

'Don't interrogate me,' she said finally, and worried that she sounded rude.

Gregory seemed unabashed. He took a deep swallow of his pint. Rosa sipped her wine.

She dreamt that she arrived in a bony, bumpy jeep at an infantry camp at the foot of Hill 24 in Southern Italy. It was shortly before the attack. She was American, a Corporal, and she was met by a young English officer. She sat behind

125

the wheel of the jeep, which was parked beside a low wall of sandbags, and was scrutinised by the Englishman with an air of repressed enthusiasm. Pink, red and blue ribbon lined up smartly on his chest, like a target. She looked back at him dumbly. 'Well,' he said, 'have you come to tell us that your boys are backing us up?' She bit the side of her lip. The shake of her head was barely perceptible. 'Oh.' He was only slightly deflated. 'Then you're giving us artillery cover? I've heard great things about your bombardments.' She found she could no longer meet his eyes. She looked over her shoulder into the back of the jeep. 'Ah,' he said, now with the air of someone making the best of a bad thing, 'you've brought supplies.' He too looked into the back of the jeep.

On the corrugated metal lay one of her canvases, one of her favourites, a salmon, silver with a scarlet sheen, leaping dynamically through a wave.

'Marvellous,' said the officer, nodding sagely, 'that's marvellous.'

'It was curious,' she told Gregory, over lunch in another pub, 'because he seemed quite gratified.'

'And why not?' said Gregory. 'Doubts about the validity of your painting, that's what it is. But your subconscious seems to be sorting them out as it goes along really, doesn't it?'

She raised an eyebrow, surprised to hear him talking in this way. He was a mystery to her. That had been one of his attractions; she liked an enigma. He was a History teacher, and she wasn't studying History. He had a red sweater that she liked and one day in the corridor she asked him where he got it. He was twenty-five, and had a reputation.

She said: 'That hardly explains the croissants. The croissants are something else.'

'Everything has an answer,' said Gregory, checking his watch. 'I have to go. I'll be late.'

Her parents weren't happy. Her dad sighed a lot, her mum asked about friends her own age. ('Carl was my age,' Rosa said, 'and you didn't like him. You didn't even like Josh.') She sometimes wondered what Frank would make of Gregory. She'd had his diary once, which might have contained clues, but she'd given it to her mum after he died, and now she didn't feel she could ask for it back. In the absence of Frank, the best place to be, she found, was Cole's studio, in front of a canvas, painting fish. He'd look over her shoulder, make her self-conscious. He was at art college now, and enjoyed sounding authoritative. 'A fish has a heart and a pulse,' he'd say, 'and something living behind its eye. That's what you're painting, not just colour and shape.' She'd grunt, and continue searching for a perfect turquoise. Then later, over tea, he'd ask her: 'So how's the aged teacher?' She'd say 'Still only two years older than you.'

Cole had got her the exhibition. He'd looked through all of her canvases, looked up at her watching him, and told her Mr Cunningham at the library would like her sort of work. Rosa had bridled at his tone. 'What do you mean *my sort of work?*' Cole had shrugged. 'You know,' he'd said. 'Fish.'

Her dreams continued. At Stalingrad the disappointment of the starving, ragged defenders that she brought no food or ammunition was palliated by the fact that she was almost fluent in Spanish. At Dunkirk they were pleased to hear that she could play backgammon. In the desert Rommel himself was amused by her imitation of Woody Allen. It increasingly appeared that she was not to be the bearer of good news, not the hero arriving in the nick of time, not the comforter in times of trouble. Her talents always appeared to be marginal to the situation as she found it. She was never, in short, the right person appearing on time in the appropriate place equipped with the proper words; never such a satisfying concatenation of rightness.

By now, Rosa was quite enjoying her dreams, but her feelings were mixed. She was embarrassed. It seemed crass to appropriate a global conflict in this way, merely to express some small, personal preoccupations. And she was frustrated. She felt that her own desires were eluding her. The dreams were like large hints that she couldn't quite catch.

Gregory had no such trouble. 'It's only natural,' he said, on the night before the exhibition, 'to take on board the cultural totems, the modern icons. Hitler. No end of people dream about Hitler. Woody Allen too. I read that somewhere.'

It seemed to Rosa that he was becoming quite fond of advancing his theories about her dreams. *This isn't your territory*, she was thinking, *you're trespassing.*

'In the absence of actual wars,' he continued, 'between nations, in the absence of disharmony between you and me, the war is occurring within yourself.'

Rosa thought this was nonsense. There was no war going on inside her, she was aware of no explosions or deaths. Except at Stalingrad, where she had heard distant shooting, there was no evidence of fighting in her various dreams. The dreams seemed to her peaceful things, generally affirmative. There was just this harmless habit of turning up in the wrong place.

She got on top of him and began to move against him. The truth is, she was pretty sure she knew what Frank would make of him. 'Artist,' he said, smiling, like it was a rude word.

All she wished for, was a little clarification.

The exhibition, at first anyway, was an unqualified success. Sipping wine and chewing snacks, Gregory, Cole and her parents and friends moved around with pleased smiles on their faces. Closing her eyes for a moment, Rosa heard no words, just a pleasant, approving hubbub, like the noise of a breeze on water. Opening her eyes, she found that a rash of small red stickers had broken out on her paintings, like measles.

That was when the pipes began to leak. The first thing Rosa noticed was a sucking, squishing sound beneath her feet, and she looked round to find that she was leaving watery footprints. Mr Cunningham, much concerned, was on his hands and knees examining the carpet, while her guests bravely pretended that nothing untoward was happening. As the evening progressed however, this became increasingly difficult. Soon they were wading through knee deep water.

Rosa looked around for Gregory, but he seemed to have become lost among the sea of strange and familiar faces. That was when something odd happened. She was standing in front of another picture of minnows, tiny wriggling things only just discernible in a dark pond, and as she watched the water lap at the watercolour she thought, *It's ruined, the paint's running, it's a disaster.* But the paint wasn't running, it was the minnows. They had detached themselves from the canvas, leaving an empty pond behind them. All around her, fish were splashing into the water with little exhilarated tail flicks, nibbling at the brightly coloured tie of the librarian, almost dancing, seeming to celebrate their liberation.

And that, as if it wasn't enough, wasn't all. As she watched, the sodden dress of the woman from the *Courier*, plastered to her body, appeared, improbably, to become too small. Or at least, the wrong shape. Her wine glass and her vol-au-vent, which so far she had stubbornly held above the rising surface of the water, floated away out of mutating hands, her hair shrivelled, her eyes shrank, and her skin silvered and scaled. She turned into a trout. Looking around, Rosa saw that the same, or similar, metamorphoses were occurring all over the room. She felt weak at the knees, a convulsive shiver possessed her flesh, she changed, gradually but irresistibly, into a salmon.

She swam out of her constraining clothes and, in the crowded pool which now filled the library, she looked again for Gregory. There he was, a small, placid looking lobster with a shiny grey shell, looking around contentedly, little black eyes gleaming. She tried to give him a wave, but of course she couldn't, and in any case she didn't fancy the look of those impressive claws. She moved away, with a few flicks of her supple body, and found herself swimming with some difficulty up the stairs. This felt right, this felt appropriate. While other fish swam in circles below, she and the salmon from her favourite painting, who had come to join her, swam up the stairs, up the stairs and away from the aimless shoal beneath her, towards the unknown but irreproachably correct destination that had not, until now, appeared in her dreams.

❧

Gregory returned all her pictures, except the crab. Cole spent the next Saturday morning teaching Rosa techniques with sky. On future mornings he was going to pass on to landscape and buildings and finally people, but he never got that far because Rosa fell in love with cornflour blue, with altitude, and with the short, tough filaments of feathers.

2002: ON THE HEART, AND OTHER MUSCLES

HE WASN'T GOING to shout at Ali. He wasn't going to slam doors or swear under his breath. He was going to search methodically, until he found it. Logic said it must be somewhere in the house. They were standing in the hall, and he was holding a short, black coat of Rosa's in some soft material. For a moment he wanted to touch his cheek to it and smell it, but he didn't. He delved in the pockets. Felt something sharp and let go quickly.

Ali watched him. That patient look. 'I'll send it on.'

'I know. I know you'll send it on. But I want to find it.'

'Fine.'

A black woollen scarf, tasselled. It wasn't in the drawer by the door. (Gloves, keys and a map of central Manchester.) It wasn't on the coat hangers or in any of the other coat pockets. (Two timetables, a sucked Polo, a list written on half an envelope.) He'd already checked his drawers in the bedroom. (Empty.) And it wasn't in the bag of old clothes he'd discovered under his bed.

'Why is there a bag of old clothes under my bed?'

Another look from the repertoire, like he was accusing her of something. 'I don't know. I don't know why there's a bag of old clothes under your bed.'

She left him to it. He stood in the hall like a man about to leave, but he wasn't about to leave. It was only a question of finding a scarf, but as he'd searched significance had somehow gathered, and the task had become a thing that had to be accomplished. It came down to this: he could not be expected to leave until he'd found his scarf.

Ali heard him blundering around upstairs. What was he doing? Was he *trying* to annoy her? She prodded her toe at the vacuum cleaner's On switch, and its hoarse growl drowned him out. She had plans for this room. Move the sofa away from the radiator, put the TV in the spare room. Things were going to be different. She pushed the vacuum up and down. You had to take it on trust that it was actually doing anything. She saw a hair, but it refused to move, somehow resisting the physics of suction. She also saw her hand, the road map of wrinkles on each knuckle. Cream, she needed cream.

She turned off the vacuum and found a tub of moisturiser on the kitchen table, where Rosa had left it when she went out. A blob on her thumb, and a slow massage into the back of her hand. Meanwhile, she listened. No sound. She wished Bill would just leave. She massaged her other hand, smelling coconut, or what passed for it. It was time he left; Steph would be arriving soon. Ali went back into the sitting room and looked around, trying to imagine the changes she had in mind. Then she grabbed the arm of the sofa and dragged it away from the wall.

The pole with the hook on the end swayed, missed, then snagged the catch. Bill yanked the trapdoor open, tugged the ladder, pulled it screeching down to his feet. Climbed up, remembering a hundred horror films where something unpleasant lurked up there in the half dark. His head and shoulders shrank slightly as he emerged above the floor. He and Ali had once had plans to convert this space into a bed-

133

room, perhaps their own, with big new skylights and an endless view of stars. Hadn't happened. The light from the unwashed window was smeary, the floor was fragile, and the dead-flowers smell of the insulation made him feel nauseous.

What am I doing up here? He'd put on a new-ish sweater today, bright red, a colour that could possibly be described as jaunty. He'd washed his hair and shaved, and given himself a confident nod and a smile in the mirror. Bristly hair, baggy but wide eyes, a pretty good colour to his skin. It had been a fairly convincing smile but now here he was in the dark, smelly attic, possibly about to fall through the floor, and he was unable to answer a simple question. *What am I doing up here?*

Sagging boxes were stacked in a corner. He pulled cautiously at one, not wanting to be buried under a cardboard avalanche. Looked inside. Fat, paperback volumes. *Rehabilitation For Cardiac Problems.* Ali's old physiotherapy textbooks. *Essentials in Strength Training.* Relics of another life. *On Muscle and Movement Imbalance.* He'd met her when she treated him for a sports injury, twenty-four years ago.

He was in the centre circle, and Marc passed to him. He hoofed it straight upfield, towards David on the wing. The ball was long gone, he was watching it, admiring his skill, when someone he didn't even see tackled him, it was like a bus running into him, and he fell into the mud, twisting his knee and screaming in pain.

Ali squeezed his leg, he summoned the nerve to ask her out. If Marc hadn't passed him the ball, if he hadn't summoned the nerve, if she hadn't said *Yes*, then their relationship would never have happened. Sean and Rosa would never have happened.

He was standing in the attic, looking at the dirty win-

dow, reliving an ancient football game. Underneath the
window, was a binbag of clothes on some old shelves. He
opened it, smelling mildew, and sank his hand into the soft,
damp tangle. It felt like organs, like he might find a liver in
here, kidneys, a human heart. His fingers closed on one
item, and he blindly pulled it out, like a child trying a lucky
dip. What if this was his scarf? Surely that would be a good
sign on this difficult day? It wasn't, it was a baby's vest. He
stepped back, and noticed that the binbag wasn't sitting on
shelves, it was sitting on a changing table. He put the vest
to his nose and inhaled, searching across years for the
fresh, propitious scent of his first child.

She had that tone which said *Don't argue with me.* 'I'm not
pregnant.'

'No?'

'I'm not having a baby.'

'OK.'

Her stomach jutted like the dome of St Peter's.

'Seriously, this whole thing is a mistake. Phantom preg-
nancy.'

'And the scan?'

'A mistake.'

'OK'

They took her in when she was two weeks overdue, gave
her something to induce in the early evening, and told Bill
to go home. He didn't want to, but they told him there was
no point in staying all night, nothing would happen till
morning, so he left, sure that he shouldn't leave, furious
with himself for leaving. He felt he was revealing a funda-
mental character flaw. He lay wakeful in bed, waiting, and
sure enough the call came at midnight. A nurse, business-
like. 'Come back. Quickly.' He jumped in the car, swearing,
and sped all the way to the hospital. He was certain he was

going to miss the birth. It was eight miles. He was certain he wouldn't make it.

Now he was cross-legged on the floor of the attic, holding the baby's vest. His breathing seemed to have slowed down. Was he suffering a cardiac problem? An imbalance of some sort perhaps. He needed strength.

'Scarf,' he said. That was all he needed. It had been a present from Ali. He hadn't seen it for weeks, but if he left without it now, it would be as if some vital part of himself was missing. 'Scarf, scarf, scarf.'

Ali imagined it lying somewhere, snake-like, in a corner or under a table. She imagined reaching down and it rearing up, sinking fangs into her hand. Perhaps Bill knew exactly where it was, and was just stalling.

She was almost horizontal, pushing the sofa towards the window, her head a foot above the rug. She could see what she'd missed with the vacuum. A small crusty particle, standing on end. A fragment of biscuit? The sofa suddenly slid away from her, and with a *whup* of expelled breath she was on the floor. Pain steamed into her lower back, like someone digging a knuckle in, just to the left of her spine. Ali gritted her teeth. Steph would be amused. *Should've stuck to physio, maybe you'd remember how to deal with heavy loads.* Ali decided not moving was a good idea. She closed her eyes. The fridge hummed into life.

Her body remembered this. Arms and legs stretched, knees and elbows locked: she was diving into the rug, frozen just before she became kinetic again, feet kicking, hips undulating, hands slicing the water. Water had been her element once, the place she felt most at home. She'd thought it was her right to win races, she'd had dreams of

136

Olympic gold. Perhaps she'd start going regularly again, she could find a senior circuit to compete in. Things were going to be different. It wasn't too late—she felt a sudden surge of excitement at this idea—it wasn't too late to swim the Channel. This had appealed to her for a while, and she'd even started a vague, unstructured training programme. Life had got in the way. Bill, marriage, work, children; but there was time now, time to rediscover what she'd once lived for.

'What do you think, Frank? You think swimming the Channel's a stupid idea, don't you?'

No answer.

'Well, let me tell you something: you're no judge of what's stupid and what isn't.'

She lay still, her cheek becoming imprinted with the rough surface of the rug. She pincered the fragment of biscuit in her fingers and wondered if it was a day old, and edible, or weeks old, and liable to make her ill.

The hum of the fridge abruptly stopped.

Bill searched unthoroughly. The last twenty-four years had been piled and bagged and tidily boxed up here. He had no wish on this particular day to root through old books and damp clothes, his nostrils full of the smell of decay, and he didn't even believe the scarf would be there, but he still searched. And when he'd searched up to a point, and didn't want to search further, he found he still wasn't ready to leave the attic, and its library of memories.

He'd barged into the delivery room to find Ali panting and gasping, and Sean's head just about to emerge from its cave. Precipitate labour. He watched, shocked, as a little human squirmed out of his wife like a fish. He'd known in theory that this was going to happen but still, it didn't seem that it could possibly be right. Ali screamed, squeezing his hand, digging her nails into his palm and drawing blood.

Bill lifted his palm and stared at it, feeling foolish. Dug his nails into it and watched the marks fade. Sitting in the attic, slightly nauseous, thinking about childbirth. He remembered Sean a few months later, shuffling on his bum around the sitting-room. Bill had moved cushions along behind him, to catch him if he fell, until Sean had reached a rectangle of sunlight and stopped, looked over his shoulder. He saw the line of cushions following him, and laughed.

If he'd had his mobile on him he might have rung Sean right now. *How are you? No, I mean it, how are you?* Could he call? *I was just remembering Sean, just remembering how you squirmed out of your mum like a fish. How I placed cushions, to catch you if you fell.* Maybe not.

Ali got tentatively to her knees, then stood and stretched her spine, feeling no more than an acceptable twinge. Still no sound from upstairs. Lately the house felt like a machine for keeping them apart, shuffling them, ensuring they settled in different compartments. Sometimes no more than a thin wall between them, sometimes two floors. Rosa, when she was home, shuttling between with her long-suffering face on, her *Don't mind me, I'm just collateral damage* face.

The sofa was now diagonally across the room. Straight-backed, knees bent, Ali lifted the vacuum cleaner and headed for the kitchen. In her poor days she'd dreamt of having a well-stocked fridge. It had been a joke phrase between her and Steph: the satisfaction of a well-stocked fridge, the joy of a well-stocked fridge. Wine and smoked salmon, Italian salami, cheese, ice cream, and perhaps a man just ready to defrost whenever you needed him. It had been Al Pacino in those days, the Al Pacino of *The Godfather* and *Serpico*.

She opened the fridge. Leaning against a tub of Flora was a green envelope, with *Mum and Dad* written on it. Rosa's handwriting. Ali took it out, along with the cheese. She picked up a few slices of parma ham, and smelt them. They were too cold to smell of much. She lifted one gauzy slice and dropped the whole thing into her mouth, just as the phone rang.

Bill heard the phone, heard the ringing stop as Ali answered. Galvanised, he climbed down the ladder and slid it noisily back above the trapdoor. Then hesitated in the doorway of his and Ali's room. Twin beds. Two wardrobes, one of them empty. He turned away, and headed for another door.

Sean's room. Radiohead poster; a still of Billy Bob Thornton looking blank in *The Man Who Wasn't There*; another poster, over the bed, of an anonymous blonde almost fellating a microphone. Everything strangely tidy. He sat on Sean's bed and picked up Sean's phone. Dialling tone. Ali had finished. He tapped in a number.

'Hello, Sean.'

'Dad, are you OK?'

'Yes, fine.'

'But really?'

He tried a small laugh. 'This is what I was going to ask you.'

'Me? I'm great. But it's a difficult day for you. For you both. So are you?'

'Am I what?'

A note of impatience in Sean's voice. 'OK?'

139

So Bill found himself in a conversational corner he hadn't planned on occupying. He was the father, surely he was meant to ask the probing questions?

'It is a difficult day,' he agreed.

'How's Mum?'

'That's one to ask her, I'd say. What are you doing?'

Sean told him about Liz and his job in the bookshop and his thoughts that possibly, he hadn't ruled it out anyway, he had a notion that he might apply to one of the London schools for a degree in Architecture. Bill chose not to pursue this, on the principle that if he pursued it, it might disappear.

'Good,' he said. 'Sounds interesting.' He had thought of a probing question. 'Do you know where my scarf is?'

'The black woollen one?'

'Yes.'

'I've got it.'

'You've got it?'

'I've got it down here.'

'That's my favourite scarf. Your mother gave it to me.'

'I nicked it. Sorry.'

'Do you know when she gave it to me?'

'No.'

'When she told me she was pregnant, with you.'

A silence, as if this needed some absorbing. Then, 'Do you want it back?'

'Doesn't matter.' And it didn't. The significance that had accrued around the scarf had evaporated. On an impulse Bill asked, 'Do you know why there's a bag of old clothes under my bed?'

'My stuff,' Sean said. 'Meant to take it to Oxfam, didn't get round to it.'

'Under my bed?'

'Any reason why it shouldn't be?'

Bill considered this briefly. 'No,' he said. 'None at all.' For some reason he was smiling now. Something about Sean wearing his favourite scarf in London, something about the bag of clothes left carelessly behind, under his bed. But any time now there was going to be an awkward silence, he could feel it coming, so he hastily told Sean he had to go. Some more assurances that he was fine. Bill was looking at the blonde singer, her unfeasibly glossy lips.

'Bye,' he said. Then added, 'Love you.'

This was impulsive. He could hear Sean's surprise in the sliver of a second that followed, containing renewed concern, the formulation of a reply.

'Yeah,' said Sean. 'Me too.'

Ali sat at the table in the kitchen, looking at lunch.

'Did you see this coming?' she said.

No answer from Frank.

'Even if you did, it's only down to your pessimism. Why were you so pessimistic about everything?'

Still no answer, obviously.

She'd begun talking to her dead brother a couple of months ago. Bill had said something casually unpleasant to her as he left the house. A new client had just spent fifty minutes complaining about her life. She'd closed the door on the client and said, 'Frank, are you there?' As if she was talking to an answerphone, hoping he'd pick up. Not every day since then, but most days, she'd had a few words with him.

'Wish you were here,' she said, which is how she usually signed off for the day.

She took a deep swallow of wine. Steph couldn't come. On the table some ham, cheese and bread, and the bottle with Rosa's envelope leaning on it. Bill entered, smiling.

'I know where the scarf is,' he said. 'And I've solved the mystery of the bag of clothes.'

Ali watched him, trying to see him with the eyes of someone who'd never seen him before. His wide face, slabs of cheeks, small mouth. His surprising smile, as if all that had really been bothering him was the scarf and the bag of clothes.

'Have lunch with me,' she said. 'Before you go.'

She'd noticed his eyes first, twenty-eight years ago. A hopeful, not over-confident gaze. She was scared of confident men in those days.

He sat, and started making himself a sandwich. She pushed the card across the table. 'From Rosa.'

A black and white photograph of some flowers. He opened it.

Sorry this is happening, but want you to know that I'm unlikely to be irreperably damaged. Still angry with you. Still don't know what's going on with you. Why can't you like each other? Is that so hard? And what will we do at Christmas?

It was signed *Love Rosa*, with two crosses.

'For such a bright girl, it's a shame she can't spell.'

Ali nodded. 'Knew you'd say that.'

'She worries me.'

'Of course.'

'I think about Frank, I wonder if it could be genetic.'

Ali shook her head, a quick, brief movement. 'No. She's unhappy, but he was in another world altogether.'

He sighed. 'I suppose you're allowed to be unhappy at her age.'

She smiled at him then. 'Any age,' she said.

They took their wine into the other room, and sat on the skewed sofa. He didn't ask why it was in the middle of the room, and she didn't mention it. They sat at an unusual angle and looked at a not often looked-at corner. It was a moment to find some formula of words, explanation or consolation.

'Do you remember giving me the scarf?' he said.

She nodded, half-smiled as she let that day return to her. 'Of course. I remember it perfectly.'

'Do you? I don't think I remember anything perfectly.'

They sipped wine simultaneously, distracted now by different but similar memories.

Bill shook his head, as if to clear it. 'I remember this moment perfectly,' he said. 'The rest is all a bit mysterious.'

They were silent, while the digits on the video changed from 1.29 to 1.33. Then he stood up.

'Just got to get something.'

She heard him on the stairs. A pause. Then he was coming down again, with the bag of clothes from under his bed.

'That's me then,' he said.

She stood. 'But we're not sorry, are we?' she said. 'About all this time?'

He looked a little shocked. 'God, no.'

She kissed his cheek to erase her question, and held the bag while he put on his coat. Then handed it to him with a puzzled look.

'Sean's clothes,' he said.

'You will be seeing them, you know. Sean and Rosa.'

'I know. I know, I know. But things are going to be different.'

She nodded. She said 'Yes.' Stood in the doorway and watched him go. Waved when he turned back to look, her hand held still at shoulder height until he turned away. Then she closed the door gently and turned her back on it, pressed her back up against it. They had been living together for twenty-six years. Now they weren't. She looked at the empty hallway, and began to assess the differentness of things. She said 'Frank, are you there?' She listened to the echo of these words for a few moments, and then she said, to the empty house, and to all of the ghosts gathered in it, 'Wish you were here.'

2004: THE DEATH OF A
FRIEND OF A FRIEND

ALI CLAIMS THEY have royal blood in their veins. She's
never tried to explain, never produced any evidence,
but she won't take it back either. If it is a joke, it's a long-
standing one.

Rosa, as she thinks of it, slumps a little, her foot slips on
the accelerator, and suddenly her car is charging towards
the van in front. She stamps on the brake, swearing, and
stops and stalls with an inch to spare.

'Fuck.'

She nods at the van driver, who is turning round, waves
weakly. She doesn't want to get into a fight. She wants to
be cool. She turns the key. The engine coughs and starts.
She begins a slow count to ten, a habit she's picked up
recently, and she gently presses the accelerator. Moving up
the queue turning right out of her road, concentrating as
she reaches the front, waiting for the gap, waiting for the
gap, and then turning the wheel, and breathing deeply,
deeply, while . . . reaching . . . the number . . . ten.

Queen Rosa. Didn't sound right. Had there ever been a
Queen Rose? You could imagine a Princess Rose, in a pink
gown, being saved by a handsome Prince. Probably not the
role model her mother had in mind. Princess Anne perhaps, because she's thoughtful, and independent, and
seems to be largely clean and tidy. No, Ali would have had
a more charismatic figure in mind. Boudicca, in her chariot, with the reins in one hand and a spear in the other.
Rosa would be Boudicca, and Sean would be Richard the

First, in his mail, with his long shield and his ridiculously heavy two-handed sword. (If Richard's sword was two-handed, Rosa wondered, how did he carry his shield?) Boudicca and Richard the Lionheart. That might please Ali.

When she thinks about her brother, Rosa thinks about the way he holds a beer glass. He gets his whole fist round it. Aggressive. Can you hold something aggressively? Sean can. She's remembering the last time she saw him, in London, in the smoky bar near his flat. They sat in a red booth, facing each other over the table. The walls and the seats were red, she felt like she was sitting inside a body part. He held the glass in his fist, and the conversation limped.

She dropped this into the silence: 'Remember how you told me that you'd always hated me?'

He stared at her, sucking on his cigarette. Short hair, squinty eyes that darted off to the bar now and then, as if he'd rather be somewhere else. Then he shrugged.

Wine. She'd better get some, and it might as well be on the first part of the journey, in streets she knows. Sunday, and the traffic is like rush hour. If there was one thing in her life she could change, it would be the traffic. Perhaps not the first thing, but one of the first. She'd abolish it, ban it from cities. Here's a space, but it's small, and there's a car behind her, and if she goes past the space to back in then the car will probably follow, leaving her no room, and if she does have room she'll probably mess it up, she'll be self-conscious with someone waiting for her to finish. Better to leave it. The car behind takes the space, while she drives on slowly, with her finger quivering over the indicator. Boudicca, in her chariot.

Trams have a superficial appeal, but those criss-crossing wires would be disturbing, and those metal wheels slicing through their metal tracks—they're unacceptable. If she ruled the world, Rosa would allow buses, run on electricity, purring demurely in narrow lanes bordered by wide, wide pavements. Large and slow-moving, like clumsy, tamed beasts.

She buys two bottles, and some nuts she'll eat as she drives, if she can open the brown foil bag. The trick is not to try to open it the way you would a packet of crisps, by pulling it apart, you must tear downwards. In fact, if you look, there's a tiny arrow suggesting exactly this. But it's difficult to do while driving, and she has already narrowly avoided one accident, and perversely the road is now clearing, so there's no convenient pause, and she'll soon be on the motorway. Her left hand is at twelve o' clock on the wheel, and she's pursing the bag between a finger and thumb. With her right hand she's trying to pincer the top and tear where the arrow is pointing. Is there any reason for the bag to be like this? Is it intended to be child-proof? Rosa drops the bag on the passenger seat. No sense in risking death over a snack.

There's a story about death current in Rosa's circle at the moment. It's a friend of a friend, one of those stories, but she did meet the man once, and she can't help but feel involved. This man, this someone who someone knew, was sitting in a pub with his girlfriend. He raised his beer and then paused, and looked across the table. He looked puzzled, and he opened his mouth as if he was about to ask a question. There was a second's silent hesitation, then he dropped the beer and fell forwards, slid down the side of the table, and landed on his face on the floor.

M621. Rosa accelerates, then brakes sharply to let a huge lorry thunder past. She moves on to the motorway behind it.

That's all, just a sudden death. But since hearing about

it, Rosa has been turning it over in her mind. Partly wondering what she would have done, if she'd been sitting opposite when this had happened. Are you supposed to beat them on the chest, give mouth to mouth? There is something called a manoeuvre, in which you heave the person up and hug them from behind. There is something else, she thinks, where you lift them by their ankles and shake them, as if you were shaking the sand from a towel. And how do you check if someone's dead? Rosa can't even find her own pulse, let alone anyone else's. And she has also been wondering what the man thought, in the second before he died, and what divided that second from the next. What happened? Where did he go?

She told Sean about this, in the red bar when they met. *Just like that, he was gone.* It was a story that was spreading out from her circle, people were telling people. *And he was only thirty.* She was finishing her meal, chilli con carne, jabbing her fork at him for emphasis. *Thirty.* Sean had shown little interest. He'd nodded and said 'Heart, was it?' before changing the subject. Sean had other things on his mind.

'See, the thing is,' he said, 'everyone goes *What are you going to do? What are you going to do with your life?* Mum and Dad obviously, but Liz too, this is the whole problem with me and Liz. What they don't get is, there's no rush. I've got potential, everyone always said so. I'll realise it when I'm ready.'

On Rosa's plate nothing left now but two kidney beans. She impaled one of them on her fork. 'See this?' she said. 'This is a bean with a clearly defined role and purpose.' She put it in her mouth, chewed briefly, swallowed. 'Now I'm full. See this last bean?'

Sean looked. It lay red and lonely on the white plate. He nodded.

'It's got potential,' said Rosa, and she flicked it to the side of her plate, and laid down her cutlery.

She moves on to the M62, and into the middle lane. The Astra in front is going less fast than she'd like, but if she tries to overtake it will inevitably accelerate, and then Rosa will be stuck in the outside lane, labouring to find some extra speed, while cars behind her flash their lights, and the one beside her refuses to give way. Rosa slows, and allows some space to develop between her and the Astra. She drives on between the empty slow lane and the busy fast lane, which looks like the traffic jam she has just left, except that it's moving at eighty miles an hour.

He'd not been impressed by the thing with the kidney bean. He'd looked at her and said, 'Anyway, how are you? I mean seriously, how are you now?'

When she thinks of Sean, she thinks of pausing outside the kitchen in his flat, halted by his confident voice.

'Oh, she's more placed . . . She knows where she is now . . . Yes, it's better. It's better. It's better than it was.'

Rosa had left the flat to buy a pint of milk. When she came back he was on the phone, talking to Ali, in tones of such authority that Rosa almost believed him. She can see him as a particular kind of royalty. Some aristocratic bully. Edward the seventh, perhaps. Wasn't he the fascist? Sean likes to think he understands people. *It's better than it was.* What had it been like before then? And what's it like now? You want to hear admiration when you're talked about, or curiosity. You don't want to hear the tone of a doctor talking about a patient, as if there's no doubt about you, no mystery.

The trip to London was a mistake. The red bar, the pint of milk, all of it. Perhaps this trip is a mistake too. She could have stayed in her little student flat, had a sandwich for lunch, or a tin of soup.

Her junction. She begins to indicate. This is the difficult part of the journey. Ali has moved. Rosa has directions, involving a park and a church and the names of pubs, but she has no map. Parents shouldn't move, they should be in one place and stay there.

Up the slip road, with the chevrons painted on it to remind her how fast she's going, decelerating obediently. It's an opportunity to try the nuts again. Rosa tugs at the bag, almost tears it in half, on her way around the round-about, and scrapes the tyre against the kerb as the contents spray out. She's nearly there, but she's not quite sure where *there* is, or where she is. Should she be on this dual car-riageway? Ali told her to look out for The Green Man at this stage. Do they have pubs on dual carriageways? Most of the nuts are on the floor, but she has tipped a handful into her mouth, and the bag is on the passenger seat, fairly accessi-ble, so really she should be calm now, while she considers turning round, if there's an opportunity to do so, when there's an opportunity to do so, and meanwhile she has for-gotten to take the directions out of her coat, which is lying on the back seat, out of reach.

Kings and Queens. The blood of royalty. How about Ethelred the Unready?

Rosa drives for a while, telling herself she might be on the right track, taking turnings, (she's late already), past the wrong pubs and inappropriate churches, and then she pulls in abruptly, turns off the engine, and gets out of her car.

Better still, some pretender who never really made it. Lady Jane Grey. Perkin Warbeck.

Veiny trees against a grey sky. It's cold. She's partly look-ing for someone to ask for directions, and partly thinking about giving up. She could go home. Hands in pockets, pulling her denim jacket around herself. She could phone her mother and tell her she's very sorry, she got lost. Or better, the car broke down. She's on a narrow grey path, with her mobile in her hand. She's approaching the middle of the park, no one in sight except a man walking his dog, and it seems the perfect excuse, it should attract sympathy and, if phrased carefully, no blame. Perhaps Ali will even feel guilty. She should never have moved. You expect to find your parents in the same place.

Things she wants.

1. Her parents to be living together, in the town where she grew up, in the house where she grew up.

2. Her brother not to be a bastard.

3. That's all.

She's walking, watching her breath steam, pressing the buttons on her mobile, when something happens. The man walking his dog stops when he reaches Rosa, glares at her, and snarls 'Hey, what do you think...?', and then pauses, seeing her for the first time, stops talking, and walks on.

Rosa stands still, shaken, and watches the man go. What was that about? Did he think he knew her? What was his problem? He's already gone, taking the second half of his sentence with him. Rosa can only watch him go, wondering what she should have said.

When she thinks of Sean she thinks of words failing, of silences, of a person talking only about himself. Look at how he changed the subject so quickly. What did he have on his mind that was more important than the death of a young man? If you believe him, there's an awful lot going wrong in his life. Girlfriend, work, and the elusiveness of something, something important. He's never specific.

'I know,' he finally said, in the red bar, 'I know you're angry with me. What I want to do is find a place for us to begin. And I know that won't happen, because you can't just start again, but still.' Sucking his cigarette, gripping his glass. 'Still, as long as nobody dies, it's possible, isn't it? A place to begin.'

She sits on the grass in the park, then lies down in the cold grass, breathing deeply, tipping her face towards the sky and counting to ten. She's looking at cloud shapes, feeling the curve of the round world beneath her, not thinking about what she's going to do next, thinking about nothing at all, (although Frank is a presence beside her, and her brother's words lie in her mind—*as long as nobody dies*—and she's not unconscious of them), just breathing clean air deeply and trying to relax, until she finally . . . reaches . . . the number . . . ten.

This could be the park she's supposed to be looking out for.

She decides to work on this assumption and see where it leads her.

It leads her to another jam.

She thinks she might be back on the right track and she wants to hoot and roll down her window and shout, but you can't do that, so she starts to count to ten again but she's too irritated and she starts instead to think about cars, and jams, the misery of cities. That was one of Frank's phrases. The misery of cities. You're walking along and you find that your head is filled, not with thoughts, not even with worries, but with noise. Cars. The mobile snarl, growl, rattle and clatter. Long slow sighs, and sudden menacing whines. Brakes groaning, like whale song. Traffic. The problem is that you can't think, or you can't move. If she could change a single thing in her life.

Death is on Rosa's mind again, and she's frustrated, suddenly she's in a hurry to get there, as if her brother and her mother might be going somewhere, she wants to hoot or shout, but doesn't. You can't do that, you have to keep yourself together at all costs, you mustn't forget there's someone else there, looking in their mirror at you, maybe angrier than you, at some pitch of rage you've never known about. Anyway a person, not a thing, someone with feelings. You find real people, and real feelings, where you don't expect them. You forget, and then they turn around and surprise you.

Rosa is arriving safely, she's accomplished the unfamiliar journey without accident. She doesn't hoot the horn or shout, she doesn't retreat with a lame excuse, she keeps herself together. Things are better than they were.

Up the gravel drive, twin furrows, crunching beneath her wheels. The gravel reminds her of the nuts, which are underfoot, and on the passenger seat, and in her pocket. Are they multiplying? They're everywhere. She stops the car and brushes the nuts off her lap, and when she looks up she sees her brother. She doesn't know it yet, but in future, when she thinks of Sean, one of the pictures that will come to her mind is of him standing in the drive, the smile on his face that usually annoys her, the anxious look in his eyes, as he waits to welcome her. And underneath it, like a soundtrack to this picture, Sean's voice, offering his tired, tentative version of redemption: *A place to begin.*

ACKNOWLEDGEMENTS

Some of these stories have appeared, in earlier forms, in *Critical Quarterly*, in the anthologies *New Writing 11*, *Northern Lights* and *Turning the Corner* and on Radio 4.